HAVE A NYC

New York Short Stories

2012 Edition

Edited by Peter Carlaftes & Kat Georges

THREE ROOMS PRESS
NEW YORK, NY

Have a NYC 2012

First Edition

Printed in the United States of America

ISBN: 978-0-9835813-3-8

Editors: Peter Carlaftes & Kat Georges

Cover and Interior Design:
KG Design International
katgeorges.com

Published by
Three Rooms Press, New York, NY
threeroomspress.com

To the memory of
Donald E. Westlake

INTRODUCTION

New York City has inspired writers since its inception. But New York City has evolved in many ways from a working class town to a tourist destination. Crime is down, streets are cleaner, fewer rats in the subway. It's as if there isn't much left of the grit and grime that made New York the setting for so many stories of the past.

Just scratch the surface and you still have the same kinds of intrigue, lust, danger and determination that have always set The City apart.

This new short story series acknowledges that the energy that drives New York is still there, and not just in "hipster" neighborhoods or well-trodden streets. New stories are forming and reforming moment by moment. Drifters pass through and lend their ideas; natives look to cling to the things they see are ebbing away; the underbelly still writhes and reels to an urban beat; and the familiar landmarks take on new looks and menace as technology slowly grips the throngs of people walking the New York City streets.

The writers in *Have a NYC* represent a range of views and styles, from longtime native New York scribes such as Lawrence Block to newcomers from far-off lands like Claus Ankersen. Many of the writers are active participants in the city's underground literary scene, which thrives out of the spotlight with a stimulating force all its own. Others are fresh, young writers, with sidelong glances masking presumed innocence.

Have a NYC offers new insight into a city that simply refuses to be swallowed by the increasing homogeny of the Western world.

Dive in and prepare for a new city view.

—*Peter Carlaftes & Kat Georges, editors*

NEW YORK SHORT STORIES

THE TOURGUIDE
BY KAT GEORGES

"And here is a box of New York's Best Cannolis, for all of us to share," the tourguide said. She held a white cardboard box high above her head. Liz was a short brunette. Neat: tailored woven silk jacket over designer jeans, urban black leather boots, well-kept nails with a fresh french manicure, chic intelligent glasses shielding deep brown eyes that took in much more than they gave away. Now she was smiling on a warm spring afternoon on Bleecker Street in the West Village. Smiling, at the seventeen tourists in her group. Smiling, in that way people smile when they expect the people they're looking at to smile back exactly the same way.

They did, reflexively. Good, Liz thought. More smiles, more tips. She glanced down and opened the box lid and carefully showed off its treasure—seventeen mini cannolis. The tourists took a few photos with their cell phones, then she gently handed them one mini cannoli each.

Tourists are so damn easy to please, she thought, over their adoring clicks and coos. Goddamned sheep. I could give them dog shit and—as long as I told them a good story about it—they'd suck it up with a stupid grin and tell me over and over how delicious it was. As if they knew from delicious. I give them the best slice of pizza in the world, they get goo-goo-eyed and gush about how it reminds them of their first slice of Domino's. I give them the best cannoli in the world? To them it's the same as some crap they "just love" from Dunkin' Donuts. They've got no ability to distinguish quality from mediocrity. As long as they're eating and they don't get sick, they love it. Idiots.

Liz reached for the last cannoli in the box and held it out without looking up. A hand reached out, fingers brushed hers as they took the treat. She heard a familiar voice. A repeat customer. She had heard it a few times during the past few weeks. A man's voice: smooth, deep. "Thank you, Liz." She glanced up. He waxed on, "I just love your walking tours. Far better than any of the others! You are amazing!"

It was not a compliment. Compliments never scared her like this.

***

He was the definition of a middle-aged man: medium height, a little overweight, slightly balding. Sunglasses in the top pocket of his striped short sleeve light blue shirt. Neat khaki pants; brown leather loafers—cheap and well-worn. He'd been on the tour two—no, three—times, always with a different woman—some dowdy out-of-towner or another. Some small-town woman past her prime. A Kansas, Georgia, Arizona type. Some lonelyheart on a weekend break from Facebook.

This time he was all alone. He smiled at her. She did not smile back.

***

When was the first time he came on Liz's Exclusive West Village Bits and Bites Walking Tour? Hard to say. These days, she ran it so many times every week. With repetition like that, memories blur. It was all rote by now: life on repeat. Jackson Pollock's first art studio was here at 69 Carmine Street! Bigtime mobster Vincent "The Chin" Gigante roamed these very streets as a child before he became boss of the Genovese crime family! Jack Kerouac sipped espresso at this very table of Cafe Reggio!

How long had she been at it? Two—no, three—years? God. Too long. Should have stuck to walking dogs.

Her first tours—three years ago—gave her that same sheer joy she had as an actor back in her little theater days. She researched her part—went to the library on the weekdays and found out interesting tidbits about the West Village that she knew would make her tour The Best. Enthusiasm flew out of her—infectious. Tour groups were thrilled. They recommended her to friends back home. She was able to go from one tour a week to four a weekend, and—by summer—tours on weekdays as well.

That first year, in July, she led at least one tour a day for three weeks straight. She was able to buy real food instead of junk. She ate out once in a while. Got her hair cut and colored at the local salon instead of doing it herself. Bought new clothes. Even shoes.

It made a difference. The better she looked, the more business improved. By the end of October that first year, she was turning away customers. By December, she had saved enough to take a few weeks off during the cold months.

Bursting with newfound confidence, for the first time in years, she auditioned for a few Off-Off-Broadway plays. In February, she actually landed a small part in a staged reading (a long and not very interesting play by a middle-aged woman from Queens). Middle-aged—like me, she thought. Everyone else in the theater scene was so much younger. Liz lied about her age on her head shot, but even knocking off ten years didn't help. Her theater days were over—except for her tours.

***

But by the middle of her second year of leading the tours, it was just another job. The kind of job you take when you live in a rent-controlled studio, don't have a lot of bills and don't want to work in an office or restaurant.

She stopped going to the library for research. History is finite—there's only so much you can learn about a six square block Historic District in New York City. She wondered how actors in long-running plays on Broadway could get pumped up for their roles after the three-hundredth performance. That's what it was now: performance. No need to improvise.

She had figured out exactly how many steps a typical group of overweight mid-Westerners could waddle without getting sore feet. How many minutes they could endure without eating another nibble from one of the cafes they passed. She figured out exactly how much water they needed—or claimed they needed—to make it through a one hour tour without fainting or whining about the heat. She even ordered bottled water with a custom label that had her website address printed under a cute caricature a friend had done for her back in the days where friends used to do that kind of thing for you.

***

Liz handed a cannoli to the man and gave him a quick "back-off" glare. He looked away, bored. Typical. She remembered the way he would say sweet things to the other women he'd been with, then ignore their reply. The disconnect. Scary.

The cannolis were gone. The tourists looked up at her, wondering what was next. Insatiable. They'd already had a slice of pizza, sampled three kinds of cheese, a fresh-baked baguette, a prosciutto ball, gelato and now a cannoli. Time to wrap things up with a bang and count the tips. Liz launched into her final spiel.

"Aren't these cannoli deee-lightful?" she purred sweetly, while the tourists chewed on their last bites. They nodded and grunted. "Told you so, didn't I? Well, un-for-tu-nate-ly, folks, that wraps up our tour for today. Thanks so much for coming along. I hope you had just as much fun as I did!" The tourists applauded. Liz beamed.

"So, as you know, a tourguide needs to eat between tours! Right now, you are invited to show your love and make your favorite tourguide a very happy lady with a dash of paper currency." The tourists reached for their wallets and pocketbooks like obedient children. The middle-aged man handed her a crisp twenty. The other tourists, figuring that was normal, did the same. The tourguide smiled sweetly, trying to cover up her shock as the twenties filled her small palm. Five twenties. Ten twenties. Fifteen, sixteen, seventeen. Three hundred forty dollars! Holy shit! She'd never made this much in one tour before. She could barely speak her final lines.

"Don't forget to tell your pals back home to sign up for the Exclusive West Village Bits and Bites Walking Tour on their next visit to the greatest city on Earth." More applause. Then it was done. Liz gently tucked the tip money into her pocket, shook a few hands, and waited for the last stragglers to ask their final questions ("Where's the nearest ladies room?" "Where can we catch a taxi?") and leave.

***

"Why are you still here?" she asked the man, who lingered after the others had gone.

"Don't you know?" He looked earnest. Liz sneered.

"Don't give me that crap about how you just love my tours."

"Aww—but I do love your tours. You are the most interesting, most fascinating, most historically accurate and most successful living tourguide in the neighborhood."

"What do you mean 'living'? Sounds like a threat."

"You really should think better of me—after I helped you score all those tips today."

"Actually, pal, I can get plenty of tips without anyone's help."

"For now," he said. "My name's Ken, by the way."

Liz rolled her eyes, then smiled sarcastically. "Goodbye, Ken," she said, and turned away. She started walking up Bleecker toward Sixth Avenue, hoping he wouldn't follow her.

He did. Of course. The creeps always follow you. It happened once before, the first year she led tours. Some out-of-towner with big expectations launched into a monologue about his "special" skills, asked her out for lunch, then a movie, then a weekend stay in his Times Square hotel room. She turned down each request, hailed a cab and never saw him again.

But this guy—this . . . Ken—ugh—stupid name . . . this guy had something else on his mind. And it felt like he would keep coming back until he got whatever it was that he wanted. And what he wanted wasn't simply a friend with benefits for a weekend fling. She better figure it out quick—without letting him know that she knew.

At the corner of Carmine and Bleecker, she waited for Ken to catch up to her, then suggested they talk in the corner park. They found a bench near the entrance and sat.

"So, Ken—," she said, trying to sound absolutely sincere. "You're right. You deserve better treatment. You've been on the tour—what?—two other times?"

"Three. Plus today."

"Ah, you're right!" Liz chuckled. "Four times in all. You know, I think that's a record."

"Thank you."

Liz purred. "I'm surprised that you're here by yourself today, Ken. You always seem to have a ladyfriend with you. From out of town . . . You're from—where?—I forget . . ."

"Cat and mouse? Must we?" Ken's voice had an edge.

"Just trying to get to know you a bit better."

"You want facts? Okay. Name: Ken Prather. Age: Forty-eight. Birthplace: Mamaroneck."

"Profession?"

"Trust fund baby."

"You don't look like a trust fund baby."

"I lied. I'm a writer."

"A waiter?"

"You heard me."

"You writing about me, Ken—huh? Is that it?"

"You don't mind, do you?"

"True crime?"

"Memoir."

"Hope they're not the same thing."

"You're getting rude again, Liz," Ken said, with a cold smile. "You're much more agreeable when you are pleasant."

Liz figured he was lying about being a writer. Maybe trying to impress her, since she mentioned so many literary figures on her walking tours. Hell, the whole neighborhood was rife with literary history. Dylan Thomas, Allen Ginsberg, Edna St. Vincent Millay all had hung out or lived in this area. Today, writers lived in Brooklyn, according to all the newspapers. No one could afford the West Village anymore, since prices skyrocketed after 9/11. The only writing most of the folks around here did was signing credit card receipts and checks.

"Where do you live now?" she asked Ken. "Brooklyn?"

"Of course," he said flatly. "All writers live in Brooklyn these days."

"Somehow, I don't believe you," Liz replied.

"You don't trust me, do you?"

"Why should I? What difference would it make?"

Ken glanced down at his hands, examined them closely. Palms first, then the backside. He seemed to be looking for something in particular, some sign or a mark or, the source of an itch. He became absorbed, seemed lost from the physical world. Liz saw small beads of perspiration form on his neck and forehead. A minute passed, without either of them saying a word. Liz knew she should just leave, but she couldn't help herself—she had to find out what just happened to him.

"Ken? Are you okay? What's wrong?" she asked.

He snapped out of his trance, and looked suddenly joyful.

"I've got it," he said, standing up. "Thank you, thank you, thank you."

And just like that, he left—walking up Sixth Avenue like a new man, like the kind of man who fits in with other men. His steps were solid, he smiled a bit. Just before he was out of sight, Liz saw him pull a iPhone from pocket and start texting without breaking stride. Yep, just like other men.

***

A week went by, then two, then three. Liz led tour after tour, but Ken wasn't there. After a month, business seemed down a bit. She figured it was temporary dip in the economy. But by the end of summer, people just weren't booking the Exclusive West Village Bits and Bites Walking Tour. Liz cut out the mid-week tours first, then started scaling back on the number of tours she led on the weekends. On Labor Day weekend, she led only one tour a day, down from three a day the year before. Something was definitely wrong.

***

She spotted Ken a few weeks later. She was sitting in the corner park on the same bench they had shared the last time he took her tour. She hadn't booked a single tour this weekend, and was desperate to figure out what happened. Ken was near the park's fountain, madly texting on his iPhone.

"Hey, Ken!" she yelled, without getting off the bench. He glanced up, gave her a little wave, then turned his back to her and kept texting.

Asshole. Liz stormed over to him.

"Hey, Ken! I want to talk to you!"

"Minute . . ." he mumbled. He kept his eyes on his cell phone screen, and kept texting, his thumbs moving like a violinist's fingers, pressing strings that made no sound.

"Hey, this is important."

"So's this," he murmured.

Liz grabbed the phone out of his hand and scanned the last few lines of conversation.

> —LOL – just booked final slot for B&B GV eTour
> —WTF? 2 mo takeover? You rock!
> —Ha! App rocks
> —:p not to mention the $$$
> —O, F—she's here.
> —Lz? Duz she no?

"Hey, jackoff!" Liz shouted. "What the fuck did you do to my damn walking tour, asshole?"

Ken looked sheepish for a moment, then stood tall and grabbed his phone back. "What tour? Doesn't look like you do much of anything now, unlike—all these folks here." Ken swept his arm toward the sidewalks. "Look at all of them, happy as could be."

"What the hell are you talking about?" Liz snarled.

"Tourists—see?" Ken mused. "Hundreds of tourists."

The sidewalks did seem a bit crowded with small groups of two and three, a family here and there. They lingered in front of the bakery the cheese shop, the bar, the old apartment building. If you looked closely, you could see most of them wore headphones or small ear buds. And everyone looked happy.

Ken gleamed. "Personalized e-tour app, can you imagine? I designed an algorithm that automatically gathers immense data for each individual user, then programs a unique user experience. They get the tour of their dreams for far less than what you charge—or should I say, 'charged'—and they don't tip anyone at the end. Ta-da!"

"You're bullshitting me."

"Still don't trust me, huh, Liz?" Ken said with a smirk. "Let's investigate."

He held her by the elbow and walked with her to the front of the bakery. A man was just finishing a mini canolli, and smiling. He listened for a moment longer, then removed the sound buds in his ears.

"Sir," Ken said. "Excuse me, sir?"

The man glanced up. "Yes?"

"By any chance, were you just using the B&B West Village eTour app?"

The man's eyes grew wide. "How did you know?"

"Lucky guess. I've heard so much about it. Tell me—did'ja like it?"

"Loved it. Fantastic tour. My wife—she's right across the street—she found out about it and I tell you what—she picked a winner. This area has so much history—did you know that Jack Kerouac used to drink coffee just up the block? I love Kerouac—bought a few ebooks of his last year. I feel like I'm following in his footsteps, can you imagine?"

"Sounds great," Ken mused. "But I'm not sure if that makes sense for me. I mean, I don't know too much about this Kerry-ac fellow. Guess I'm just not really much of a reader. Oh, well. . ."

"Wait—that's okay, buddy," the man chirped. "My wife's like you—well, not exactly, of course." He and Ken laughed. Liz brooded between them. "See, my wife is more into food—if it's edible and sounds interesting, she is all over it. She's what you call a 'foodie,' see?"

Ken nodded, "That's me."

"I knew it. Well this app knows just what you like—it took the both of us to the same places, and we each found out just what we were interested in. She found out about food, and I found out about those beatnik things, and it was just like magic. A total win-win for both me and her."

Liz felt sick. She had to say something. "Wouldn't you prefer to have a real tourguide?"

The man stared at her with a curious look. "This is real."

"I mean—human. A human tourguide, who could talk and answer questions and point out interesting things and give you free samples and . . . stuff like that."

Ken and the man glanced at each other and laughed.

"I got free samples galore! And I ask all the questions I want. Here, let me show you." He held his cell phone out, turned it on speaker and asked, "Where's the nearest subway station?"

A female voice replied, "If you're headed back to your hotel, Mr. Felton, turn around, and walk up Bleecker to Carmine, then turn left on Carmine and walk three-hundred-fifty feet to the West Fourth Street Station. Take the A train to West Forty-second Street. When you get there, I'll guide you to your hotel."

"Thank you," the man said to the phone.

"There's a train in four minutes," the phone replied. "If you like, I can contact your wife across the street, and let her know that it's time to go."

"That's okay," the man said. "I'll linger here a little longer."

"I thought you might," the phone said. "Enjoy yourself."

The man put the phone away.

"Cute, isn't it?" the man told Liz. "And it's never wrong. The difference is trust. A machine—you can trust. It makes all the difference in the world."

"What about the food?" Liz snapped. "Who gives you the samples?"

"Oh, that's the great part," the man grinned. "If I want a sample at any place, I just text 'Sample please.' And the cool thing is, they know what I like and they know what I'm allergic to and this cute little number pops open and hands me the perfect sample for me and my wife. She got a chocolate éclair here. Me—I'm allergic to chocolate, so I got a cannoli. And what a cannoli it was! Best in the city, so I'm told!"

Ken glanced at his iPhone. "Well, guess I'm just going to have to find out for myself. Thank you, Mr. Felton."

Liz wasn't finished. "Wait—this is just a tour, and you trust your little app more than a live tourguide, right?

What's next? Dog walkers? Teachers? Political leaders? I mean—how far is this going to go?"

"Who knows?" the man said. "Babysitter? Lifetime tourguide?"

"You got it!" Ken said. "Those apps just keep getting better and better!"

Ken and the man looked at each other and burst out laughing.

"So long, Mr. Felton," Ken purred. "Pleased to meet you."

"Same," said the man, already texting his wife across the street, who waved.

***

Liz drifted away. Her rent was due in a few days. If she was careful she could live off her savings for at least three months, maybe four. She wondered how long it would take to learn enough to make her own app. Something that destroyed all the other apps. A killer app. That's what she needed. That's what she would become. A killer app—one that everyone would trust—for the rest of their lives.

BELLE

BY CLAUS ANKERSEN

It took me three weeks to find it. The flat on the Lower East Side. Three weeks of daily working through Craigslist, trying to find a nice, affordable place. Belle advertised a one bedroom furnished sublet in Alphabet City, and when I saw her ad pop up among the thousands rolling thru the site, I was instantly charmed. Beautifully-decorated with antique furnishings, European poster art and a classic library, her apartment sounded like the perfect base for exploring the city. I explained that I was a European artist visiting the city to work. After a lengthy email correspondence we agreed on terms and shortly after I took off for New York City.

The premonition hit me as the yellow cab slowly drove up East Second Street. Something was wrong. And indeed, on a glass pane just inside the wrought iron double door leading into the narrow building I spotted a yellow post-it note. Belle, it said, had to leave for upstate New York to attend to urgent family matters. She recommended a nice hotel not too far away, promised to reimburse me for my costs and promised to meet me the next day around noon. Slightly disappointed I accepted the inevitable and checked in for the night.

Next day at noon, she met me in the doorway. I was struck by the sadness lingering in her eyes, her too-white complexion, beneath the ghostwhite powder pancake of full face make-up. She was beautiful, sad and from the West Coast. She said "Dude." Unmistakably West Coast. There was something ghostly about her, as if she was only an apparition. Yes, she was a ghost—but she was still very much alive.

We talked for a while. She begged me to go for lunch and return in a couple of hours, to give her time to clean out her stuff from the apartment and tidy up a little. As we talked, we walked into the mouth of the building and turned left to a brown metal door next to the staircase leading upwards. She looked like she was on the run somehow, and as we entered the apartment, she explained that her good friend had kicked her boyfriend out for being on heroin, and that she was moving in with her friend to be with her in her time of trouble. Just inside the doorway was a background of scattered boxes on a coffee table, a narrow darkish room with burgundy walls and a smell of gas. I agreed to go to lunch for a couple of hours while she cleaned up, paid her the rent, the two-hundred dollar deposit, got the keys and left for sushi at the yellow corner place on Seventh Street.

When I got back from lunch, the boxes were gone and so was Belle, but not the gas leak. The gas leak remained, making the ill-lit studio-style living room seem even more sinister. I settled in nevertheless, setting up my writing gear on a small table by the only window, which opened onto a little concrete-paved backyard area. I was already feeling inspired by the city's magnificent energy flow. For the next two days I paced the blocks of Alphabet City, crisscrossing streets, jotting notes, watching people and doing write-ups in late afternoon, only to venture out as soon as I was done, surfing the city's energy and also being fueled and amused by discovering the brass plaque outside the building. "Welcome to The Croton," it read, then went on to explain how Allan Ginsberg used to live in the very house I found myself in. How fabulous was that, I thought to myself. Nothing is coincidental. Not even coincidence. What better place could I've possibly ended up in, than Ginsberg's old crib. I was so excited that I procrastinated on the gas leak for a couple of days more, then finally called Belle.

It took a while before she picked up. "Ah, don't worry about it," she said. Her voice was a little coarse. She asked if I wanted to go out for a beer as soon as she got hold of the landlord. Better, she explained, that she dealt with the landlord directly since the sublet wasn't entirely legal. OK, I thought. For the next few days, I busied myself wading around the stream of life flowing by in the streets.

When I called her next time, she didn't pick up.

After a couple of more calls, I started looking around the apartment. I found three things. On the wall next to the doorway leading from the main living room into a walk-in wardrobe redecorated as bedroom, hung a terrifying etching of a shiny black Christ, dark and foreboding, almost malicious. No—definitely malicious. Pupils placed straight in the middle of the eyes so that the damned thing looked at whomever was in that room—all the time.

Cursingly. Accusatorily. Why would anybody have an evil Jesus hanging on a hidden wall? I asked myself. Below the etching was a wooden dresser and behind that, the two other items I found: A letter addressed to Belle in a green envelope. A Polaroid of two people dancing.

I kept calling her in the following days. Her unavailability fed my curiosity. It wasn't long before I opened and read the letter that had slid down behind the wooden dresser. It was from her sister in California. It was a desperate cry of love and worry, talking about Christmas presents and mending old sibling rivalry. It seemed Belle's dad was in jail out there for a good long time, and that the sister was worried she would lose Belle too. "Please Please call me," it ended. I wondered if the sister looked anything like Belle.

The Polaroid was a snapshot that looked like it was taken in some kind of basement. A parking garage maybe. Bare. Gray. Hard. A blonde, white-skinned, skeleton-skinny girl raved around with a dark haired man, their long hair swinging, faces turned away. Junkies dancing. The dance of the dead. Living ghosts. They both looked ethereal, on the brink of dissolving into thin air, the unreal unravelling.

Was Belle making up the story of her unfortunate girlfriend? Was it really about her? Was she the heroin addict? Father was in for manslaughter. Could have been her mother, I thought. Or another sibling? Had she even been there at all?

At nights I slept on the couch in the living room, preferring the stench of gas to the presence of Evil Jesus glaring out his etching on the other side of the bedroom wall.

On the corner of The Bowery and East Second Street, one night, some days later, I ran into the Atlantean Time-Traveler operating his cart of native Indian-American Tex-Mex style on-the-go-foods. Usually you could find him there on Tuesdays. As I approached the street-kitchen I joined Hannah and her dad.

Hannah, was a proud and hungry five year old, sitting on her dad's shoulders. Her dad, a Jewish New Yorker in his fifties, ordered chicken wraps from the Time-Traveller, and asked me to take their picture. In this instant it was a given that Hannah would one day become President of the United

States. Her dad explained how she was conceived on 9/11, and how he was afraid knowing he would someday lose her to time and trajectories. The Atlantean prepared their food, while I thought of 9/11 and agreed with Hannah's dad that something good is always to be found in the seemingly evil. His mother was born on 9/11. So was mine.

The Time-Traveller proceeded to reflect on the magical nature of numbers and the miracle of all things; the number of stars on the one dollar bill, the hidden Freemason wisdom of the building forefathers of the nation. "The stars are the stars of David," said Hannah's dad, taking his leave, while the future President of the United States munched away high on his shoulders. The Time-Traveller handed over my wrap. "You never know who you'll meet," he smiled. "An alien. Or a Time-Traveller."

As my stay came to an end, I was confident that Belle would materialize—if for nothing else—just to get the keys for the apartment. But she never did. Belle was gone. Just gone. A year later, upon returning to the city of dreams, I managed to track down and contact her sister, still in California. She had no contact with Belle either.

If you ever need a good place to write in New York, let me know. The Croton might be the place for you. I still have the keys.

And if you mind Jesus—sleep in the other room.

THE WRONG WOODSTOCK

BY LARISSA SHMAILO

Nora lied a lot; she told elaborate and peculiar lies. Nora had an imaginary boyfriend who was twenty-six and beat her; she'd lost her virginity in the sixth grade; she'd been to the Woodstock festival and the Apollo theater. She'd experienced a lot for a thirteen-year-old girl from Queens.

Nora was born in Williamsburg, Brooklyn. Her family moved to Middle Village when she was a year old. Whenever people asked her where she came from, Nora answered, "Brooklyn: Williamsburg, Brooklyn."

Nora attended a school for girls in Manhattan, commuting by bus and subway every day from Queens. From where she waited for the bus in the morning, she could see the red-tinged skyline of "The City," as people from Queens called Manhattan. She'd been commuting to Manhattan for almost two years now, since the beginning of seventh grade, and the sight of the skyline filled her with yearning.

Queens, on the other hand, was the valley of ashes: Nora has read *The Great Gatsby* and blushed to realize that the grey, ominous, soulless land described by Fitzgerald as the valley of ashes was her home. Queens was a horrible, embarrassing place to live. It went without saying Zelda Fitzgerald wouldn't live here or know anyone who did. Archie Bunker lived here, and other vulgar men: racists, minor characters, people with no imagination lived in Queens. Cemeteries, packing plants, two family houses— her parents thought this was a wonderful place to live.

Nora's friend Joey was also from Queens, but from further out on the Island. She was a well-built girl with a big nose and bad skin; she wore long, torn jeans that trailed over her boots. Joey's real name was Melissa Feldman, but it didn't matter: When she talked, you could almost hear Janis Joplin singing "Piece of My Heart." Nora and everyone else at school considered Joey profoundly cool.

Joey lied extravagantly. She'd slept with John Fogerty and had helped him write "Proud Mary," and had jammed with Taj Mahal at the Fillmore East. Joey had taken mescaline and acid, all kinds—purple haze, orange sunshine, white cross, blotter, even the mind-blowing brown dot.

Shy and bookish in Queens, Nora became funny and extroverted in Manhattan with Joey. She told Joey about Steve, the twenty-six-year-old Queens guy who loved her so much he actually beat her in fits of jealousy. Joey just nodded and smoked Nora's cigarettes.

Nora liberated things from stores that year. She was finally caught at the Third Avenue Woolworth's. A young Puerto Rican guard gripped Nora's arm as she watched Joey move smoothly down the store aisle and out the exit. The guard took Nora down to a small office and made her empty her handbag. The cheap makeup and candy bars she'd lifted spilled out onto his bare gray desk. The guard wrote down her name and telephone number; he told the sobbing Nora that he wouldn't call the police this time, but that he would call her mother. Nora would have preferred it the other way around. She waited in agony for the dreaded phone call. It was months before she realized that the guard had only meant to scare her. She never shoplifted again. But Nora would have gone to the Women's House of Detention for her friends.

Nora left early for school each day to meet Joey in Central Park, taking the EE to the Fifth Avenue stop. At the entrance to the Park, she walked down the steps to the duck pond. Joey was already there, drinking coffee and feeding the ducks potato chips. Nora joined her, dropping her big, floppy bag on the rock, and pulling out her hairbrush and cigarettes. The girls sat together quietly, smoking and watching the ducks as Nora brushed her long hair.

The late spring morning rarefied the park air, illuminating the paths and trees with the kind of clear light ordinarily found only at high altitudes. Sunlight and shadow played over the rich new greens in the water, on the phosphor necks of the ducks and the opaque algae, on the grass and the leaves. A smell of horses wafted from the hansom cabs. The drunks on the benches woke up and energetic mothers wheeled their little children to the zoo. Earth Science and Mr. Pumpy's homeroom seemed small and far away.

Nora felt a stabbing pang of anxiety—suppose she couldn't intercept the postcard from the attendance office this time? Suppose they called her mother?

Nora looked at Joey, who was placidly chewing a peanut butter sandwich. Her friend's face betrayed no fear of authority, no craven need to conform.

"I'm going to cut," Nora announced to no one in particular.

"Okay," Joey agreed.

Leaving the rest of Joey's peanut butter sandwich for the ducks, the girls packed up their gear and headed uptown toward the Bethesda Fountain and the boat lake. Nora carried Joey's guitar with pleasure, proudly displaying its battered case covered with skulls, roses and Grateful Dead trucking insignia. She hoped people would think the steel stringed instrument belonged to her. Swinging west, they approached the long aisle of park benches at Poet's Row. Nora tried not to be obvious as she looked over her shoulder for the tall red-haired man. She winced as she recalled the incident. The first time Nora had met the tall red-haired man, she was with Joey. He was walking his dog, cleverly named Tripper. Tripper, an intelligent and friendly black terrier, was born at Woodstock, on the third night of the Festival. The man, a musician, regaled the girls with stories about Hendrix and the Who, the Doors and Janis Joplin. Each time they met, the red-haired man told the girls the story of his little dog's birth and baptism at Yasger's farm; entranced, the girls listened like children to a beloved fairy tale.

One morning Joey met a guy and went off to smoke a joint with him; Nora, left behind to watch their school bags, knew that the boy had not invited her because she was fat. It was then that the red-haired man came by, walking Tripper; he stopped to talk to her. Nora was thrilled; the red haired man had ignored her until then, concentrating on Joey, who was thinner and cooler looking. The red-haired man was especially friendly today, asking her questions, and remarking how mature Nora was. He asked her how old she was. Nora, who was thirteen, usually said fifteen, but today told the red-haired man that she was sixteen. To her surprise, he invited her home for tea. Nora hid the book bags, and went with the man to his apartment.

Nora could not overcome a feeling of disappointment when she first saw the red-haired man's apartment. The apartment was small and shabby, cramped and dirty around the edges. When she used the bathroom, she saw that the red-haired man lived with a woman—the makeup was dusty, the creams and tampons too much at home to belong to a casual visitor. She squelched her disappointment.

Nora returned to the small grainy living room and sat on a mattress draped with Indian cloth. The man poured her a glass of wine, and filled a pipe of hashish. Nora pretended to drag deeply, but didn't inhale for fear of coughing and acting like an idiot.

The man gently but firmly shoved Nora back on the faded bedspread. He tried to kiss her, but could not get his tongue in Nora's mouth. Nora tried desperately to relax, to go with it, as the man was suggesting, but could not: whether it was the hashish or the wine, Nora's teeth clamped shut, and would not open.

The red-haired man made annoyed noises. Disoriented, Nora staggered to the door, feeling clumsy and disgraced, praying that Joey wouldn't somehow find out.

A girl in a paisley dress stood on the bandshell stage, singing to the empty rows of chairs, as Nora and Joey cut under the street to the Fountain, and climbed to the west side of the boat lake. A wooden pier stood at the edge of the lake, hidden from view by a large, dramatic willow. The little structure, shaped like a house with no walls, held two facing benches; four people could sit there. Teenagers kissed there at night. Nora loved the little pier; she felt less anxious here. At the pier, she enjoyed the park. She forgot her mother, forgot how many classes she'd cut this year, forgot everything about home and school.

Nora had cut over half her classes this year. She had been a good student, was still pulling good grades, and, despite everything, the teachers still liked her. At parent-teacher conferences, the teachers still told Mrs. Nader that Nora was gifted girl. Mrs. Nader had always enjoyed parent-teacher conferences. Her huge bulk swelled with pride. Unable to listen to anyone for more than a few moments, she would interrupt the teacher and begin describing her own rigorous education in the Soviet Union. A high school degree there was equal to college anywhere else. At home everyone read. So it was logical that dearest Norachka, or Nora as the teachers knew her, was a good student, given her home environment.

"Good example, good nutrition," she'd conclude, as the teacher nodded uncomfortably.

But nowadays, Mrs. Nader did listen, contritely, as the teachers described Nora as a behavior problem. She still got good grades, but she didn't come to class. When she did come, she was late, or disruptive. Lately she even argued with the English teacher. And then, a truly aberrant incident: Nora threw an inkwell at Miss Taffeta, the seventy-three-year-old art teacher. Nora claimed she wasn't aiming at her, but the old lady was terrified.

Joey was playing "Suzanne." She stopped often to tune her guitar and puff on her cigarette, which she kept in the neck frets of her guitar and carefully repositioned after each drag. This made for frequent interruptions, but Nora sang with feeling anyway as leaf shadows danced across Joey's face. When Joey grew tired of playing, she surrendered the guitar to Nora, who played A minor chords.

A tall boy in a fringed jacket with a flag on the back approached the pier. Nora looked away and sang louder as the boy listened. As she started to strum the minor chords for "The Cruel War," the boy cleared his throat.

"Can I hold your guitar?" he asked politely.

Joey and the boy passed the guitar back and forth, playing Beatles songs, blues riffs, and anything else they knew. Red faced, Nora sat next to the boy, singing too loud. She didn't want to seem desperate, like her friends from Queens. If one of her girlfriends from Queens so much as talked with a boy, Nora heard about it for weeks afterward. They sifted and sifted through casual, unimportant conversations that clearly meant nothing, nothing at all to the boy: "Then he smiled, and I think he thought I meant I liked him . . . What do you think he meant when he said his school was nearby? Do you think he likes me?" Dee Ann Distefano called every "Miller" in Queens to hunt down a boy she talked to once; when she and Nora finally got her boy on the line, Dee Ann got scared and hung up.

Girls from Queens were bores. Girls from Queens were awkward and shy. Girls from Queens were vulgar and loud. Girls from Queens wore their sweaters too tight, wore too much makeup, wore the wrong kind of pants; their faces were zitty, and their tits were too big. Girls from Queens turned out like their mothers . . .

Some boys in a rowboat were calling to the boy in the fringed jacket. Nora watched the longhaired boys stand straight up in the rowboats, then belly flop into the lime green algae. The boy in the fringed jacket explained to Joey that his friends had dropped acid cut with speed. He lit a thick joint and offered it to Nora, who coughed until her face turned red. Joey politely interrupted a story about Eric Clapton to wait for Nora to finish coughing.

Embarrassed, Nora ran to the lake and threw herself into the water fully dressed. She heard applause and hoots behind her. She swam, cold and embarrassed, thinking, I have a pretty face, prettier than Joey but I am fat and my breasts flop in my wet shirt. I am embarrassed: it is too much to throw yourself into the water dressed in Central Park, it isn't hot enough in May and my jeans and shirt and shoes will take too long to dry . . .

School was letting out when Nora returned to the pier. The boy with the fringe jacket was gone. A small, hardened looking man with blue eyes and thick blue-veined arms was holding Joey's guitar. Joey was smiling stupidly at him. Nora stood knee deep in the water watching them, shifting her body back and forth as though she needed to pee.

"All I know," the man was saying, strumming the guitar, "is that the lady was thirty-seven and I was showing her things she should've been showing me . . ."

Joey laughed. Nora joined Joey and the man, smiling woodenly. The bantam man took Nora's hand in his, trailed his middle finger across her palm, and introduced himself as Rick. Rick had been to Mexico. He spoke at length about Woodstock and San Francisco and hitching. He had even been to Marrakech.

Nora saw that Rick was coming on to Joey, and that Joey liked that. The man looked like a bum to Nora. He seemed more hustler than head; there was something suspicious about his short hair. Nora detected a faint Brooklyn accent under his southern drawl, like the smell of day-old booze.

"So . . . ," Rick grinned, putting his arm around Joey's waist, "What do you girls want to do?"

Joey giggled. Nora felt anxious. She searched her mind for a good reason to go home.

"I guess," Rick drawled, reading her mind, "y'all wanta go home." He pulled on the word, making it disgusting: "Hoohome."

"We want to go to Haight-Ashbury," Joey said suddenly, her voice sounding high and strained. "We want to go to California on bicycles."

Rick paused, taken aback. He squinted at Joey, weighing her possibilities. After a moment, he smiled. "You're shitting me," he concluded amicably.

Joey, suddenly shy, looked down her big nose. "No," she said as Nora's heart sank into her bowels, "No, that's what we want to do. Go to Haight-Ashbury. On bicycles."

Rick grinned like a proud father. Still holding Joey, he put his tattooed arm around Nora. "Well, honey," he chuckled, not believing his good fortune, "That's just what we'll do."

Nora smiled numbly as Rick and Joey planned their trip to San Francisco. The idea to run away from home had taken force swiftly and suddenly, changing Nora's world with a word. She stood listening and nodding, wet and miserable in her damp sneakers. The day was supposed to be ordinary: she was due home for dinner, she would watch *Star Trek*. Then Joey had made this stupid joke, and the stupid joke was now a dare. Nora could never refuse a dare.

"The first stop," Rick explained as they walked down Fifth Avenue, "is East Third Street. My friends have a pad on East Third. We can stay there till we get the bread for the bicycles."

Crowds of unsmiling office workers pushed out of their offices into the subway. Rick panhandled, mocking the people who gave him money with his servile tone.

"You girls could work for a couple of weeks," he suggested. "I know where to get papers easy. Most of the time, girls like you don't even need papers to work." Nora was uncomfortable, but was too conscious of her breasts bobbing beneath her wet tee shirt to notice much else.

Joey was in her element, grinning and greeting Rick's marks with a peace sign and a power salute. Nora walked quietly, keeping a little apart, feeling as though she didn't want to know where they were going.

They turned east on Fourteenth Street. The girls followed Rick to the door of a large building, Salvation Army Headquarters, waiting for him outside. After a few minutes, he reemerged with blankets and a can of peanut butter the size of a gasoline drum. Nora felt ashamed, as though she had stolen something from a very old poor person. Laughing too loud, she accepted a blanket from Rick, wrapping it around her shoulders like a cape.

Still, Nora was surprised: apart from a small nagging feeling of guilt, she felt pretty good, even excited and happy. There was momentary remorse as they entered the East Village where old, hobbling, wrinkled Ukrainian women walked on Second Avenue. Left behind to die by their ungrateful children, thought Nora. But when they passed, she immediately felt better. Nora was surprised—she'd expected to suffer more.

Night was falling and night gave Nora a sensation of freedom. She had never been to Manhattan after dark before. Roaming the East Village in the company of her peers, free and unconstrained by a fat, domineering woman telling her how to walk, talk, act, dress, eat, sleep, think, look and feel, Nora was enjoying herself. There would be changes in her life now, she thought, finally, painful but necessary changes. The idea filled her with excitement and dismay.

Feeling happy, Nora began panhandling. As they passed the Fillmore, Nora drew the army blanket close around her. She stood under the marquee, laughing and reaching her hand out to the crowd with a flourish.

"Alms for the morally handicapped," she called, finding encouragement in the disapproving looks of the older people.

Joey and the others chimed in cheerfully. "Alms for the morally handicapped," they howled. "Alms for the morally handicapped."

A passing young man smiled and pressed something into Nora's hand. To her delight, she saw it was a dime.

The crash pad was not what Nora imagined: it was shabbier even than she'd expected, a walk-up furnished with discarded mattresses and crates. The pad was next door to Hell's Angels headquarters and was secure; the Angels protected their own, Rick said. There was a broken window and no door. A defunct kitchenette without oven or refrigerator connected the two small rooms.

Rick introduced the girls to the pad's unofficial leader, a leathery young blond man named Mike. Mike slept in the front room in a makeshift loft with Mary, a plump, dreamy girl who was five months pregnant. A tall lanky man named Chris who worked nights at the docks slept in the loft during the day. Rick, Nora, and Joey made camp on the floor with Kenny Sunshine, an acned young man who spent his days shooting crystal meth and his nights talking and crying.

The inhabitants of the crash pad seemed vague and enervated, lacking the energy Nora expected from the counterculture. They were politically apathetic, which shocked Nora more than a little. Neither Mike nor Mary seemed to understand the basic issues of the Vietnam War, even though Mike had scrawled "Nixon, pull out—like your father should have" on the bedroom wall.

No one paid much attention to the girls. Joey fit right in, making herself useful by cleaning and dishing out the

Salvation Army peanut butter. Nora felt uncomfortable, but tried not to show it, remembering Queens.

By tacit agreement, Mike was in charge of the pad and its inhabitants. As the admitted father of Mary's unborn child, the seventeen year old assumed a mantle of authority that caused the older men to defer to him. Mike was slight, a wiry junkie with sleepy eyes. He wore gold religious medallions when they were not in pawn, and had actually been taken for ride by an Angel on his chopped hog, a mark of extreme favor that Mike was careful not to presume upon.

Every day at noon Mike brought home three cases of beer. Presiding over the distribution of the six packs, Mike sat in the loft with Mary, drinking tall boys and instructing the girls in the code of the street.

"Respect," Mike said, nodding significantly. "I show respect for people; they show respect for me. That's beautiful." Mary and the girls smiled beatifically. After a few beers, Mike insisted upon respectful treatment and Mary made special efforts to avoid any affronts to Mike's dignity.

Nora's first night, Rick staggered into the outer room clutching a bottle of malt liquor. Seeing her there, he took a sudden sexual interest in her. Shoving his unshaven face into her cheek, he took her hand and pressed it to his crotch.

"Ya wanna get me off?" he mumbled.

Nora was dimly aware as Rick grabbed her breast that this was the first time he'd ever spoken directly to her.

Nora lost her virginity to Rick that night in the empty outer room. The splintered floor was dirty and cold, and she was on the bottom. Rick was ready and she didn't have time to put down a blanket. It hurt. It hurt terribly. She tried not to cry aloud but couldn't help it, couldn't stop crying because it hurt so much. She kept hoping it would be over, but it went on, and she bit her hand, trying to muffle her cries. She knew that Joey and the rest were next door and could hear her, hear her clearly. Now Joey would know that she'd lied when she said she'd had sex before. Now they would all know what Nora had always suspected was true: that she was frigid . . .

The next morning Joey said, "It was your first time, wasn't it?" Nora nodded, burning with shame.

The next night Rick slept with Joey. He ignored Nora, who thought this was appropriate after the way she acted the night before. It was just another vitally important thing she'd messed up. Nora slept with Chris, the dockworker in the loft that night. He was gentle, and Nora was glad not to feel anything.

Nora was returning from the East Street Mission with food for the pad when the Hell's Angel Mario called her over. Terrified, she crossed the street slowly.

Mario looked Nora over.

"How old are you, kid?" he asked.

Nora froze. She looked at Mario: the Angel's bullish eyes were bloodshot.

"Twelve," she lied.

Mario closed his eyes and fell silent, lost in thought. After a long moment, he opened his bovine eyes.

"Can you go home kid?" he asked.

Nora was taken aback. "Sure," she said.

The Angel held her cheek between his fingers and shook his head sadly.

"Go home, kid," he said. "Go home."

The girls went home after a few more days. Joey called her sister who said there was a thirteen-state All Points Bulletin out for the runaways. This was standard procedure for missing persons but the sound of it impressed Nora.

Joey was determined to stay. Nora held out a few days but finally decided to go home. Joey felt betrayed and disgusted. "You'll tell them where I am," she sneered.

"I won't, I won't," Nora swore. Panhandling the price of a token, Nora rode the EE to Queens and walked the bus route home to Middle Village.

The Naders were in mourning. Convinced Nora was dead. Mrs. Nader refused to believe that her daughter could leave away from home of her own free will. When Nora arrived, her mother hugged her, and immediately called a gynecologist to look Nora over.

Nora never knew what the doctor had told her mother, but Mrs. Nader told Nora she was still "all right down there," and to make sure she didn't tell her father anything.

"It would break his heart," Mrs. Nader insisted.

Mrs. Nader blamed Joey for Nora's running away, despite Nora's protests that she had chosen to run away of her own free will. Mrs. Nader considered Joey an especially pernicious influence and spoke of the girl with genuine hatred.

"The little bitch hates her mother," Mrs. Nader would say, almost spitting as she talked. "Listen to how she talks about her mother." She veered her bulk on Nora. "And you talk the same way, telling everybody what a bitch your mother is."

Nora tried valiantly not to tell her mother where Joey was, but Mrs. Nader grew more furious.

"The love of a mother for her children," Mrs. Nader screamed, "is the most powerful love on earth, a love more powerful than you will ever know. Because," Mrs. Nader proclaimed, "you don't love anyone."

Nora held out until the day Mrs. Nader ended a tirade by collapsing on the kitchen table. As she lay there, moaning and clutching her heart, Nora told her the address of the crash pad. Mrs. Nader sat bolt upright, looking at Nora like an alert raptor. Nora thought she discerned the hint of a smile.

The Naders soon began to refer to Nora's "adventure."

"My troublemaker," Mrs. Nader said affectionately, "Since you were small you have always found some mischief to get into. When you were little I would say to Olga, 'Go look next door, Nora is too quiet.' And your father—how your father loved you. Every night he woke you up to play with you. 'Nikolka,' I would say, 'don't bother the child.'"

Mrs. Nader started telling the neighbors that her daughter had a lot of Huck Finn in her.

When Nora and Joey were allowed to go to school again unchaperoned, they decided to run away to the Woodstock commune. Joey had fallen in love with Kenny Sunshine, the speed freak. Now Joey wanted to follow her man to Yasger's farm, where they could work the land and love freely.

Having betrayed her friend once, Nora felt obligated to accompany Joey now. On the day chosen for the runaway, Nora left for school in a skirt to mislead her mother. Her family was abnormally nice to her that morning. Her father spoke to her. Her mother stopped her as she was leaving. She kissed her and called her little sun, small chicken, dearest, dearest little daughter.

"You are such a good soul, small one." Mrs. Nader looked proudly and lovingly at her daughter. "Come straight home from school, I'll have dinner. Okay, dotsinka?"

Nora nodded, feeling treacherous as she hid her jeans in her book bag. She took eleven silver dollars, coins her grandmother had given her before she died and the only money Nora had, and wrapped them up carefully so they wouldn't jangle. A feeling like heartburn mingled with her tears as she left home, never to return.

Joey and Nora hitched out of New York City. In her poncho with her breasts covered, a trucker took Joey for Nora's boyfriend. This misconception pleased the girls; after the first ride, they no longer tried to set the drivers straight.

Joey was better equipped than Nora. She carried a sleeping bag, thermal underwear, and even an extra blanket for Nora, who had only the clothes on her back, jeans and a short-sleeved shirt. Joey took charge of the map, deciding the route and rests. They stopped the first day by the side of Route 22 in Jersey or Pennsylvania; Nora wasn't quite sure what state they were in, but hesitated to ask. They camped and dropped acid by the side of an industrial stream.

Nora had never taken acid. She sat patiently, heart beating, waiting for something to happen.

Joey moved first. "We are not getting off. We've been ripped off," she said angrily.

She gave Nora another three hit tab of purple haze. Nora saw the colors play on Joey's neck as Joey chortled, "The sun . . ."

For Nora the stream is covered with spider webs, she can't walk, her legs are dead and can't move can't walk can't be afraid the worst thing is to be afraid so scared she wants it to stop that's wrong that spoils everything . . .

A fish is struggling in the webs she is walking she is caught across the stream the leaves of trees are moving like small squares on pendulums, tick-tock . . .

Nora realized with embarrassed horror that Joey was feeding her cold beans to bring her down.

> *Jeans don't dry fast it is cold in May to sleep outdoors in wet jeans on stones near streams in sleeveless shirts it is cold . . .*
>
> *Big Man comes barreling out of a fast car moving down the highway like a streak in the night. He tumbles and falls onto the shoulder of the road, rolling down the grass fast and drunk. He lands like a billiard ball on the knoll where Joey and Nora sleep. He lies down on top of Nora, making himself comfortable . . .*
>
> *Nora lies about her age again: "Please don't do this to me mister I'm only twelve years old. . . ."*

They came to Woodstock. It was a small town and there was a parade going on, a patriotic parade. The drum and bugle corps was marching down Main Street. Young girls were playing glockenspiels. Young men in crew cuts and uniforms were pulling the town cannon down the street to general applause. Nora and Joey were in Woodstock, Vermont; it was Flag Day.

* * *

Nora and Joey hitched back to Woodstock, New York but Mrs. Nader was already there. Against her will, Nora ran out from the woods where she was hidden. "Moma," she cried.

* * *

Joey's mother put her in a psychiatric ward in Jamaica, Queens for eight months. When she got out, all she could talk about was the hospital. Joey became the social pariah of the ninth grade. Nora decided she would try to be a better student and daughter. One of her classmates, a girl with hairy legs, confronted her in the hall.

"I really looked up to you," the girl said quietly. "I really did."

At the parties she went to, and to anyone who would listen, Nora would often relate the anecdote of how she hitched to the wrong Woodstock.

FIREFLY
BY ADAM R. BURNETT

I was in love again. She was the love of my life. I could not imagine a day without her. And in New York City this happens often.

Her name was Fanny and on our first date we shared a cigarette in the middle of the street. She leaned against me, laughing in abandonment. I was surprised at how unguarded she seemed around me. Like I had always been there, next to her, sharing a cigarette. I had heartburn and couldn't stop belching. And this is my newest compromise. I used to get through a night without burping, but in recent years I only expel more gas and I expect this will only worsen with age.

In the middle of the street, after a barrel of beer and two cigarettes, I kiss her on the lips. She pulls away. I pause and then swiftly shake her hands. She laughs, her dimples beaming, turning from pink to red. She steps away and curtsy into a laugh, my god she's so gorgeous but I know I've done something terribly wrong here.

"Sorry, the handshake was a mistake," I blurt.

"A mistake?"

"I don't know what I'm doing."

"I would never admit that to anyone. Especially someone you just kissed."

"Dammit. That's the worst thing you could have said, too."

"Well, maybe we should just say goodnight then."

"No, no, no. That sounds awful. Let's just wait a bit, to cover that up."

"You think that's a good idea?" she squints. Does she want me to kiss her again? I go in and she stops me. "Eek! Oops. No. That's not what I was saying."

"Of course not."

"Sorry."

We sit down on a bench in silence, there near the Bowery. I quell up a comment, "Is that a full moon?"

She throws her hair back to me, "What's that?"

"Oh, it looks like the moon is waxing."

"How do you know if it's waxing or waning?"

"There are charts. But mostly, I think it's a matter of trust."

"It doesn't look quite full. I'd say it's waning."

"Don't be so pessimistic."

We stare at the moon, which is either waxing or waning and reserve room for our incident, and chew non-sequiturs to fill the void. Eventually the silence breaks with a shared gasp of breath, bringing us out of the prolonged dually inflicted torture. We then hail separate cabs and bow to one another, departing the scene. She—to Queens, the borough of mixed flour and abundant sunshine. I—to Brooklyn, the borough of leftovers and pork rinds. I think of her as I move through the streets, away from her, gracing the Brooklyn Bridge looking back at the city and I marvel, as I always do. You can marvel in disgust, with sweeping tones of appreciation, or with grandeur romanticism, but however you marvel it's a kneeling, an infinite respect, a silenced fear, a shaking piousness. People visit the city daily and I often forget this as I make my way from station to station, from stop to stop without considering that everyone here is not an inhabitant. It is the travesty of its existence, that there are those who only spend a few days, or few weeks or months and leave thinking they know her; that they have been in her. This is an insult, for anyone who claims America as his or her national identity ought to endure living in New York for some time. To merely visit is an affront to the city. She is not a tramp. You do not spend just a night or two with Aphrodite and Medusa, you spend years shaking, solving, loving, twisting, fighting, approaching her throne time and time again; to treat her, to treat New York, to treat her any other way is a slur to her existence.

Days pass and these days feel like weeks because Fanny is on my mind. I wake up and smoke cigarettes through these day-weeks, something I never do. I smoke a cigarette on my walk to the train remembering our shared cigarette on that now fossilized precious evening. I leave half of my cigarettes unsmoked in memorial, in recognition of a love I am already funeralizing.

And in the midst of becoming officially addicted to cigarettes, she calls me one evening. She invites me over. But there is a catch; at the door she tells me she is having mice problems. "They kind of just showed up," she says. "And now, well, they're here. They like, think they live here now."

"How many are there?" I ask, craning my neck into the apartment.

"Two or three. They're little. They don't even run away from me they're so small."

"Would you like me to do something about it?"

She cringes a bit. "What does that mean?"

Growing up in and around Capital City, Kansas, where field mice run rampant into homes throughout the winter, one quickly becomes desensitized to doing what needs to be done. There is nothing quite like a frying pan and some muscle. During a foray living in Jazz Capital, Missouri, with musicians, whose pizza boxes piled into a luxury high-rise for mice, I fashioned myself into a brutal mouse-killer. I would creep down to the kitchen in the middle of the night and catch them in their dirty scurry. In my reign as Mouse Killer in Jazz Heaven I murdered over a dozen mice. And when the luxury high-rise pizza motel was finally demolished, an entire infrastructure of pathways and nests were found. I could have murdered many more and my blood boiled at the prospect. The mice community knew of me throughout the tri-state area and after my escapades of bloody proprietorship in Jazz Heaven, I was never bothered by mice again. Until this night with Fanny.

"Do you have any pans?" I ask.

"Why? Are you going to cook them?" she laughs.

"No, I'm gonna, take the pan, and, you know, squash it."

The blood drops out of her face. "Are you serious?"

"What would you like me to do?"

"I don't know."

"Wait," I stop in my tracks, considering she might have ulterior motives, "do you want me to solve the mouse situation? Or am I over here for other reasons?

She looks at me, dull, as if I said the worst possible thing that could be said. "Other things?"

I trip on myself and fall on the floor to change the focus of the scene. "Oh how clumsy of me!" In my idiotic, feeble attempt to distract I have actually injured myself, arm is cut clean from the sharp edge of the rickety dinner table. I swiftly cover it up with my shirt. I can't overreact; she will be turned off if I start hyperventilating over a cut. "You might want to go into the other room," I say, as if warning for an impending violence only suited for adult male audiences.

"Why?"

"I'm going to take care of the mice."

She exits, hesitantly. My god, she's gorgeous.

I open the cupboard. They're all there quivering and quaking, confused newborns. In fact, there are three of them, three blind mice. My blood curdles, euphoria for the days in Jazz Heaven bubbles to the top, the exhilaration of late night murder spells, cornering the pests and railing away at them. I grab for the nearest pan. They squint, their little black eyes, saying, "Mister, how do you find food and a mother?"

One after the other, I slam them into the cupboard floor. I do it so quickly, and might I mention adeptly, that I am certain none of these day-old mice felt a thing. As I release my arm from the last mouse the scream begins. I look back and there is Fanny in the door way crying. I lift the pan. "I had to do it. What else would you want from me?" She points at me and screams. "Sorry." A dismembered tail hangs from the body of the pan. I shake it off into the garbage. Drops of blood hit the linoleum floor. The blood from my arm has begun seeping through the shirt. .

"Are you bleeding?"

"From when I fell. The table."

"Is that mouse blood?"

"No no, it's my blood. I swear!"

"I can't do this."

"Do what?"

"You killed them? You really killed them all?"

"I don't know. Is that what you wanted?" Should I kiss her? No, don't do that. That's stupid.

I go in to kiss her.

"Whoa. No, no, no. Are you kidding me?"

I wait. I bring my hand out. "Handshake?" She looks at my hand. "Well, you don't have a mice problem anymore."

"I think you should probably leave."

"That makes sense."

I still see Fanny, sometimes. I wonder if I hadn't killed those mice how our relationship might differ today. If I hadn't kissed her. If we hadn't shared that divine cigarette. I choose any number of moments in our relationship that is still prevailing. Still constantly awkward.

SHIRAZ
BY DARLENE CAH

Shiraz didn't expect to see the Cuban dancer so late. It was nearly ten o'clock, and though the commuters at Penn Station had thinned out, he still commanded a decent crowd.

At a bar across from his impromptu stage, she observed his footwork, undulating hips and trance-like gaze. He wore black. Dangerous, she thought. She was in a red mood today. Red mini. Red headband. Red lipstick. She liked the contrast to her coal black hair with its white streak and her deep-end-of-the-pool blue eyes.

She took a sip of her Corona and swallowed hard, hoping it would ease the tension in her shoulders. She'd smoked a joint with her boyfriend Mitchell at his loft less than an hour before. Still she couldn't unwind. Her new paintings, mixed-media portraits of musicians and dancers, filled her mind. Now, she pictured the dancer, in a swirl of vibrant colors, a mix of acrylics, gritty sand, shredded cocktail napkins, dimes, pennies and nickels.

His partner, joined at the hip, bent with him. Tonight she was a redhead, a life-size, soft-sculpted doll with long curls, long legs, short ruffled skirt and stiletto heels, a look of permanent ecstasy painted on her face. Shiraz wondered how it would feel to glide effortlessly, to be held in his arms, twirled and dipped. Bodies so close, hearts beating together to the music. In reality, her body created a chaotic rhythm of its own when she tried to dance. Mitchell once said she looked like she was being electrocuted. Cool, she'd thought.

The music ended and the Cuban selected another tune. The Tango. Shiraz often hovered on the fringes of the audience, wandering, but always watching. She felt she knew him as intimately as she knew the palette knife and paint that would define him on canvas. This would be his last dance tonight.

She joined the remaining onlookers as the dancer floated across the floor, a rose between his teeth. He dipped his partner and tossed the rose. It landed at Shiraz's feet.

She looked toward Track 20 as her train was announced, and pictured the night ahead, the pacing, chain smoking, as she tried once again to start the last painting in her series. She thought about the sketches scattered around her studio at home. She wanted to burn them all.

The final call for her train. Shiraz picked up the rose and walked to the dancer.

"Thanks for the rose," she said twirling it between her index finger and thumb.

"My pleasure. I see you here almost every night," he said.

She was surprised he'd noticed her, but pleased.

"I live in East Rockaway," she said.

"Then you have missed your train." He smiled and lifted his doll onto his shoulder.

She shrugged.

"Who's your date?"

"This is Cristina, and I am Alvaro."

"Alvaro," she let the "R" trill just as he had pronounced it.

"And you are?"

"Shiraz."

"Shiraz. An odd name for an Asian woman."

She took a deep breath and ran her hand through her hair, the white streak settled in a spray across the left side of her pale face.

"So what will you do until the next train?" Alvaro said his grey eyes steady on hers.

Shiraz looked around. A homeless man, wrapped in a blanket, slept against the gate of a bakery. A group of Knicks fans stumbled out of the bar. The Dunkin' Donuts and the newsstand were still open.

"Hang out in there," she said, waving the rose in the direction of the store, "Read *Cosmo* or something."

Alvaro laughed. His teeth glistened against his dark caked-on makeup.

"I saw you more the *Vogue* type."

Alvaro motioned with his head toward the Dunkin' Donuts.

"My treat," he said

Alvaro ordered and returned with a tray. He sat next to his duffel, the doll atop.

They picked at their doughnuts. Shiraz eyed the slumped doll.

"Where do you get your dolls?" she asked, breaking off a large piece of doughnut and crumbling it.

Alvaro wiped sugary glaze off his fingers with a napkin.

"I make them," he said.

She was impressed.

"Where do you get your ideas from?"

As soon as the words came out, she wanted to bite them back. She hated when people asked her that.

"People I meet. Places I go. I performed at a resort in Mexico. When I came home, I created Cristina," Alvaro said, and reached over to replace a stray lock of the doll's hair.

Tender, Shiraz thought.

"Now, Beatrice," he said, "I made her after seeing a lounge act in Vegas."

He wiped his mouth. A streak of make up smeared the napkin.

"She wears a purple evening gown. Sequins. Hair up . . . " He gestured with his hands about his head.

"Like a French twist?"

"I don't know . . . up."

They caught each other's eyes and laughed. He was older than she'd figured.

"I took her to Mexico," he said.

"Must have been fun explaining that to airport security."

Alvaro nodded. Shiraz stirred her coffee.

He stared at her, and Shiraz recognized the look she practiced often. He seemed to be memorizing the shapes, angles, light and shadows of her face. She turned away.

"How long till your train?"

"Few hours," she said, mashing doughnut crumbs with her index finger.

"Come. I live nearby. We can talk more comfortably."

"Oh. No, that's all right. There's a waiting area."

She wadded the remaining doughnut in its wrapper. Alvaro got up, and lifted the doll.

"I understand," he said, "but I thought you'd like to see my dolls."

He glanced at a sketchbook in her tote bag.

"Talk. One artist to another."

Shiraz thrived on risky situations. Last year, she had sat

alone in the Second Avenue subway station at two-thirty in the morning, absorbing the sounds, the colors, watching football-size rats scavenge the tracks. A twitchy kid, no more than nineteen, staggered down the stairs, and sat next to her. She could have moved away, but she stayed. He pulled a cloth-wrapped package from his jacket.

"I hunt," he said.

He laid three knives on his lap then held one in front of his face, and told her about the deer he'd gutted. Still she sat. When the train arrived, she left him licking his dry lips. She sketched for days with little sleep until her vision vibrated to life. The resulting freakish deer paintings earned her a corner in a Williamsburg gallery. Risk was vital to her work. This sudden hesitancy terrified her.

Shiraz caught up with Alvaro on Eighth Avenue. The rose in her hand was beginning to droop. Nice, she thought.

Alvaro's apartment was a two-room studio in a six-story walk-up. The hallway smelled of mold and cigars.

When Alvaro opened the door, Shiraz saw their faces, vacant eyes staring. Thirteen of them on a bench along the far wall, each with a different hair color, expression and costume, their names on index cards taped to the wall. Angela. Sara. Michelle. Alexandra. Beatrice, with her purple gown and upswept do.

"My harem," Alvaro said and propped Cristina among the other doll dancers.

Shiraz brushed the rose against her face. They were like spirits. She kicked off her shoes, sat and let the deep wing chair embrace her. For the first time that day, she relaxed. She was intrigued that she could feel at ease in a stranger's apartment. Within the tenement walls, pipes clanked and the steam radiator by the window hissed. She visualized a canvas splashed with thick gray and blue brush strokes, peeling, sloppy, almost edible acrylic paint, against a wash of orange flecked with bits of glossy black, and the dolls' eyes, dark like holes in the canvas.

Alvaro returned, and the rose slipped from her hand to the floor. He had changed into a white tee shirt and jeans, and his pompadour was combed smooth and wavy. She noticed the deep wrinkles at his eyes, another traversing his forehead, and a shiny scar above his right eyebrow. He sat in a chair opposite her.

They started to talk at the same time, but his question hung in the room.

"So what is your real name, Shiraz?"

She twisted her lips.

"My Japanese name is Chika. It means a thousand summers. I hate summer."

"In my country, chica means little girl," he said.

"Well, there you go. Wrong in two countries," she said.

"And your parents? They don't mind you changed your name?"

"I don't have parents," she said, scanning the white walls and ceiling, up to the milky translucent light fixture, its bottom dotted with dozens of flies, martyrs for seeking the light.

"I'm sorry."

"They're not dead," she said, "I just don't have them."

Shiraz swallowed. Her mouth was gummy dry.

"I was born here. I have my art. They're stuck in the past. Like I would go back to Kyoto with them. Marry some fat banker and paint pretty watercolors between popping out babies. Right. Totally not me."

"So you want love," he said.

Shiraz picked at a loose string on her skirt.

"Please," she said rolling her eyes and thought of Mitchell. Brooding, manic Mitchell.

"Parents want what's best for their children."

"Then they should be happy. I'm doing what's best for me."

Shiraz glanced at the dolls. This wasn't going as she expected. She should make some excuse. Get up and leave, but now she saw Alvaro in brown monochrome alternating thin washes of tempera with thick, chalky chunks of paint and plaster, stippled black and red enamel, strips of newspaper obituaries and gold leaf crosses.

Alvaro got up and selected a CD. The room filled with a pulsating Latin beat, accented in suspended syncopation by congas and claves.

"Do you know the Rumba?" He extended his hand.

"Oh God," she said with a snort, "I don't know how to dance."

"It's easy. Come." She remembered her fantasy of being swept across the floor in graceful movement. With an exaggerated sigh, she took his hand and allowed him to pull her out of the chair, to draw her close.

"Now," he said, his posture perfect, "Right foot back. Left to the side. Right meets left. Slow. Quick. Quick. Like this."

Her choppy steps were a rude counterpoint to Alvaro's moves.

Shiraz tried to disentangle herself from his hold.

"I'm not a good follower."

"You just have to learn to let go," he said, and he gently nudged her into a turn then reeled her in.

"See?" His breath warmed her face.

Her gaze wandered to a tattoo on the inside of Alvaro's forearm, a red rose in a tangle of thorns. The rose wept teardrops. Or was it blood?

He let go and walked to the kitchen. Shiraz spun away and met the dull eyes of the dolls. She imagined them mocking her, heads together, hands over their mouths.

Cristina, the redhead, leaned against a brunette with short curly hair. Next to her sat a blonde with straight hair knotted into a bun topped by a tiara, then Beatrice with half-closed eyes and the type of a smile that knew a secret. Shiraz scanned the dolls until her eyes rested on a small table.

A low flame from a votive candle danced in the dark corner. Pictures of the Virgin Mary and Saint Lazarus flanked a photo of a woman and two children—a boy, Shiraz guessed to be about twelve and a younger girl. Rosary beads draped the frame.

"My wife and children."

Shiraz startled. Alvaro stood behind her.

"You're married."

"No," Alvaro said.

Shiraz gazed back at the picture. The flame reflected on the glass.

"I'm sorry," she said, as if she were in church.

Alvaro nodded.

"Rosa. Beautiful wasn't she? Lovely dancer, graceful, powerful."

The flame cast a glow on Alvaro's face. Saint-like, Shiraz thought. He told of their fantasy to leave Cuba and dance with an American company.

"That's Lazaro, and my little girl, Luz. She would be nineteen now."

Shiraz shook her head.

"I don't understand," she said.

"I bought a boat. If we could get to America, I could dance. I could give my children a chance at a good life."

He told how the boat was crude and the sea turbulent, how Lazaro was pitched overboard and how he strained to grasp his son's outstretched hand, fingertips just out of reach.

He told how Rosa struggled to her feet, how her empty eyes met his for a brief moment before she turned to stare at the sea, how he felt her arm slide along his, not even trying to grip, as she tipped over. He told of Luz shivering, her lips blue, eyes glassy.

"The shore was so close, I could see buildings," he said, "I held Luz close to my heart, but she was gone. Fifteen years, this week."

Alvaro started back to his seat. "Luz means light, you know."

Shiraz felt a trickle of sweat slither down her neck.

Alvaro rested his head on the back of his chair.

"The dance was in her soul, my Luz. She would see the street dancers and imitate their moves. So passionate. So innocent. Every night I would count out the steps for her."

He lifted his head and locked eyes with Shiraz.

"How many dreams did I destroy for my own?"

"You wanted what was best for your kids," she said.

The words sounded muffled in her ears, as an image of her father flashed in her mind, his soft round face, his gentle hands, guiding hers as she grasped the pencil and scratched her first lines on paper.

On her seventh birthday, he'd come back to the States from a conference in London and held out a package. She tore at the paper and squealed at the sight of the tiny tubes of Winsor & Newton watercolors. Cadmium Yellow. Viridian. Alizirin Crimson. Her father kissed her forehead.

"Paint me a summer garden, my Chika," he said, and she promised she would.

Alvaro shifted in his seat, shaking Shiraz from the memory.

"I should go," she said.

"No, stay. It's late. It's not safe."

Alvaro took a blue blanket from the hall closet and Shiraz curled up in the wing chair. He tucked the blanket around her, and placed the fallen rose on top.

"The blanket matches your eyes, Chika," he said and headed to his alcove bedroom.

Shiraz looked at the dolls, her eyes unfocused. They were a Greek chorus revealing her secrets, fears and desires. She imagined herself a doll among them. She thought of Mitchell and wondered if he would care that she was sleeping in a strange man's apartment. She hoped he would.

When she closed her eyes, it was Alvaro she saw. Alvaro, a realistic rendering, now in fluid uncontrollable watercolor washes. Alvaro, in translucent streaks of blood red, ocean blue, fiery orange and warm terra cotta, swirled in graceful motion.

THE SPECIALIST
BY DAVID R. LINCOLN

From the scar on the back of my hand, you can see I've lived on the islands. North of Canal Street, in the memorial rich Mars Bar. Where I discovered Lisa one morning three days later, after I hit the shores of New York.

She was framed by The Three Irish Terrorists, as they all called themselves. All three of them living a subterranean existence these last seven years on the Bowery, the entire time appearing in only a half dozen low-key restaurants.

The Mars Bar was recreational. Edith "The Man" sat balanced on a bar stool, at one end of the bar where the TV monitors offered her shade from the scrutiny of strangers. The screen was to distract unwelcome attention, so they could recreate.

Her companion, a goat-faced anarchist, appeared to be looking out to the ends of an extremely distant galaxy. A sad oasis of recriminations on a bar stool, brown spikes of a tumor protruding from his forehead, he amused her with his jokes.

"What's the difference between fishes and apple pies?"

Edith twitching her vague smile in anticipation.

"Apple pies don't start screaming," Edith's friend said, "when you poke a hot tire iron in 'em."

I watched her whinnying laugh. It spun her around so she almost slipped off the barstool.

"What is seven times seven?"

"That's easy. Fourteen."

"No, it's fifty-six," their suave Errol Flynn mustached companion said impatiently. "How many times do I have to explain it to you? Over and over, honestly you make me sick."

They were absorbed in themselves in the corner, hiding in the dark shadow under the TV set, as I said. I was curious about them. I had a notion that they hovered wherever they could find a spot of relative privacy for a few minutes. A prudent move for any self-respecting stranger.

Errol Flynn and I continued our conversation on Hemingway from before.

"Hemingway understands killing," he said darkly.

Lisa, I could see, did not belong with them. She had only appeared on that bar stool by accident, because of an unfortunate tendency that attached itself to her all too often, these days. When we first met, she still dressed with style, but that was seven months ago. A touch of class was yet evident in her pearl earrings, her red satin skirt and her black tennis shoes. The perfume on her neck, which I remembered from the last time we spent together, sloshing around the island, made my head swim. She had surprised me how long she could last on speed; she didn't appear so very strong until the wee hours of the morning. Having a look at the sky! We were two grateful freaks spending the whole day together for an entire week. Her arm braced on the boozy wheel of circumstances, all the time, driving from the proverbial wrist. And I remember how great she looked, walking along the esplanade in Battery Park, wearing her expensive jewelry and offering to take me to New Jersey to meet her mom.

"So, I haven't seen you here in a while."

"It's been three months, twelve days, and six hours since I was in here, which must have been the last time," I said.

"Since I saw you."

There wasn't anything to tell. I had been in my usual whirlwind the entire time. Two times to San Francisco. Once to New Orleans, then here. I was entirely like I am, still, today, as I've been ever since I discovered it is a viable proposition, to live like this. Racing around like a thief. Always full of spectacle and the important events of the day. Not all of them flattering, I might add. Meanwhile I could see time passing in the faces of these people, they changed from trip to trip. It was like watching an old black and white movie when the hands of a clock on the wall start spinning around, or a vase of flowers blooms, withers and collapses in a matter of five seconds. So I saw these people mired in their grounding, epicene reality, the syntax of mistakes and beauty marks etched into smiles and frowns.

Kind of like a turkey festival.

Sorry if that insults you. (Checkout the mark on the back of your hand.)

"The islands are beautiful this time of year," I said.

We never disagreed on too much. The main thing was the turpentine smell of soul thinners around the bar. I'd stop for a moment and listen to myself talking, I could barely distinguish at times when I was on or off; I knew one thing, these days more people were saying things similar to what I was thinking myself. That was alarming. At times I even felt diluted.

"How long are you here for anyway?"

"I don't know. Maybe Wednesday. I haven't figured out what I'm doing at the end of next week. Don't worry, something always happens."

"You like surprises?"

I'd had this realization a few months ago, while sitting on the banks of the Mississippi, what brought me here was to see how the dandelions were doing in May. The more places I kept track of, the more places I had to keep up with, how they were doing. It gets to be a problem. Seriously, everything is always evolving its own weird artifact. Just to see how weird it gets, you have to take another look. Maybe that's why I was always suckered by a woman in a low-cut blouse.

"It's nice to find people who can still talk," I said.

"We are civil. If you want to commit suicide then you have to step outside of the Mars Bar."

The polite laughter of the Irishmen sounded strangely familiar. Like I might have been standing in the same place for too long already.

The last time I spoke to Errol Flynn, he revealed to me certain sensitive information about him and his friends. The Three Irish Terrorists were waiting on a mission, and until that time came, that they should be called upon, they would remain alert, in case that time came. That they were to be called on.

"Seven years," he'd said. And looked bitterly into his pint glass. When your time came, people said you sensed it because you began to think about your enemies with sadness. That you might never see them again. No more time to complain about the way things were. You lived to follow the signals.

"When you're a professional," he said, leaning forward with his handsome face, "you catch your mark in his sleep, so it can be a surprise. The class way of doing it. You tap him on the nose, the bridge of his nose, with the weapon barrel, you wait until it's there in his eyes, the memory of who you are, and why he is about to die, and then you blow his head off."

He was probably good at his job.

"You're probably good at your job," I told him.

Errol Flynn didn't try to deny it.

"It's important to keep an edge," he said. "That's style. That's what professionals have that amateurs lack."

I switched to Lisa. Lisa was always a sweet-hearted chick to me. I never knew what to say when she told me how she liked to pass the time. She failed to notice that I was nervous, or it didn't seem to bother her. I could stay longer, one of these visits, we could shack up for a while, except there were too many sharks in the water, too much going on here in the reef of freedom.

"Why don't you come to my cousin's art gallery opening tomorrow night?"

"Where is it?"

"You know, we've been there together."

She tossed the hair off her back.

"You mean, above the pool hall on Ninth Street."

"It's on the third floor," she said. "We watched the haiku of busses at the corner. They all made perfect noise."

The strange thing about this was how much of it I couldn't remember. But I always had a sense of what was coming. When you're watching the shadows in the eyes of all these half blind people, it's a kind of miracle that any of them survive from one trip to the next. There was a kind of curious longevity that beat all the odds, these personalities. Which was part of their fascination, I suppose, why the mark on my hand was a burning sensation. After I'd seen them cussing and hustling and drinking themselves sick, until the light off the walls in this establishment made them all appear half dead, I would come back and they'd be just who they were. Mostly aware of the surrounding indifference.

"All men are killers by nature," that Irish dodger Errol Flynn was saying.

There you go. The guilt was in the nature.

I'd wanted to see Lisa again, after the last time. I suspected I knew exactly what she really wanted. And I never would give it to her. She was always too trusting, a little too nice with everybody. I would read a magazine and fondle her leg for the longest time, absentmindedly, while she examined the messages on her little blue purse phone, with the genuine abalone coating shell. She read an entire issue of *American Plumber Magazine* while I was running my hand up the svelte inside seam of her thigh, waiting until I was ready to discuss building an actual relationship.

The two on the stools were still arguing about math. Lisa was stuck in the middle. Squirming happily under the lights of the bar. Exactly the way she liked it.

"Gio," she said, "don't you remember?"

I didn't want her feelings to be hurt.

"Sure, hon, I remember. The haiku thing was great."

"You start with the second line first," she giggled, voraciously—I'd seen her tittering like a school girl too—Gio—"

When she touched me, I stopped listening. A girl like that, it soothes her just to talk. What's the point if she starts talking? She does it to hear the sound of her own voice. Even if she has to suck it up to The Three Irish Terrorists in the Mars Bar, that's better than staying home and having to not call her mom, or some fuck. Whatever it is, I knew the score, Lisa was like a lot of girls between here and Chicago and between Chicago and Memphis, after a couple drinks she had a load of stories. She was a veritable trove of stories, in fact. The last time I stayed in her place, after seven days she said it was our week; she had to make a point out of it at the end, that it was our special time. And who knows, maybe she was right. I can confess right here that I might have thought I might run into her in the Mars Bar, from prior occasions that we hooked up. Now I'm back to, what I used to call it, my little pleasure island hat trick.

"Those are great times," I said.

"Are?"

"Well, we can just pick up where we left off."

Lisa, folding her bangs away from her eyes, for a moment, blinked in a non-discrete, showy way.

"You really think we can just, like, occupy the same space for a moment like that? Whenever you want to?"

"I don't see any reason why not."

Lisa considered this for a second or two. She was an intellectual person. She was also quick to laugh in the face of any philosophical position you might try to pull on her. Only, you'd never hear that kind of laughter, she'd sit there with a finger on her chin, considering the odds and the risks, the chance that I might have picked up something since the last time we slept together. In fact she was damn good at figuring me out. She was sweet and I wanted to consider losing my head over her, at least once.

"I'm sure there's something we haven't seen together," I added suggestively.

I wanted to absolve her of all possible responsibility, from the start.

Lisa smiled from the rim of her cocktail glass.

"Now you're giving me a line," she said.

And she knew where she was with that. It broke her in half. She was in heaven. She smiled in anticipation of the next pebble on the complex series of steps we had to cross in order to make it up to each other, for the last time, the moment of tension at the end. That little burst of sunshine every time I waved goodbye and stepped on the bus at Port Authority. It was enough, I would tell her an hour later when we got back to her place, to see the unicorn decals on her double bolted door. To keep me wondering what I had to do to see her again. If I was free to go. Go where the weather suits my cold.

Like every line, ultimately, the references only bothered me when I couldn't complete the thought, where had I heard that?

"About those apple pies," I said, turning to the nearest person on Lisa's right side. "How hot was that poker?"

Lisa laughed elegantly, going along with the tide. Errol Flynn was going on about Hemingway and how he was his favorite writer. The two on the stool were looking ghoulishly wrecked, like two condemned people determined to enjoy themselves for as long as possible. And me, drinking my tonic water and lemon, spending as much time as I possessed, occupying the place I liked best of all, right here in the heart of New York City.

I try not to miss anything that happens, ever.

IN FOR A PENNY
BY LAWRENCE BLOCK

Paul kept it very simple. That seemed to be the secret. You kept it simple, you drew firm lines and didn't cross them. You put one foot in front of the other, took it day by day, and let the days mount up.

The state didn't take an interest. They put you back on the street with a cheap suit and figured you'd be back inside before the pants got shiny. But other people cared. This one outfit, about two parts ex-cons to one part holy joes, had wised him up and helped him out. They'd found him a job and a place to live, and what more did he need?

The job wasn't much, frying eggs and flipping burgers in a diner at Twenty-third and Eighth. The room wasn't much, either, seven blocks south of the diner, four flights up from the street. It was small, and all you could see from its window was the back of another building. The furnishings were minimal—an iron bedstead, a beat-up dresser, a rickety chair—and the walls needed paint and the floor needed carpet. There was a sink in the room, a bathroom down the hall. No cooking, no pets, no overnight guests, the landlady told him. No kidding, he thought.

His shift was four to midnight, Monday through Friday. The first weekend he did nothing but go to the movies, and by Sunday night he was read to climb the wall. Too much time to kill, too few ways to kill it that wouldn't get him in trouble. How many movies could you sit through? And a movie cost him two hours' pay, and if you spent the whole weekend dragging yourself from one movie house to another. . .

Weekends were dangerous, one of the ex-cons had told him. Weekends could put you back in the joint. There ought to be a law against weekends.

But he figured out a way around it. Walking home Tuesday night, after that first weekend of movie-going, he'd stopped at three diners on Seventh Avenue, nursing a cup of coffee and chatting with the guy behind the counter. The third time was the charm; he walked out of there with a weekend job. Saturday and Sunday, same hours, same wages, same work. And they'd pay him off the books, which made his weekend work tax-free.

Between what he was saving in taxes and what he wasn't spending on movies, he'd be a millionaire.

Well, maybe he'd never be a millionaire. Probably be dangerous to be a millionaire, a guy like him, with his ways, his habits. But he was earning an honest dollar, and he ate all he wanted on the job, seven days a week now, so it wasn't hard to put a few bucks aside. The weeks added up and so did the dollars, and the time came when he had enough cash socked away to buy himself a little television set. The cashier at his weekend job set it up and her boyfriend brought it over, so he figured it fell off a truck or walked out of somebody's apartment, but it got good reception and the price was right.

It was a lot easier to pass the time once he had the TV. He'd get up at ten or eleven in the morning, grab a shower in the bathroom down the hall, then pick up doughnuts and coffee at the corner deli. Then he'd watch a little TV until it was time to go to work.

After work he'd stop at the same deli for two bottles of cold beer and some cigarettes. He'd settle in with the TV, a beer bottle in one hand and a cigarette in the other and his eyes on the screen.

He didn't get cable, but he figured that was all to the good. He was better off staying away from some of the stuff they were allowed to show on cable TV. Just because you had cable didn't mean you had to watch it, but he knew himself, and if he had it right there in the house how could he keep himself from looking at it?

And that could get you started. Something as simple as late-night adult programming could put him on a train to the big house upstate. He'd been there. He didn't want to go back.

He would get through most of a pack of cigarettes by the time he turned off the light and went to bed. It was funny, during the day he hardly smoked at all, but back in his room at night he had a butt going just about all the time. If the smoking was heavy, well, the drinking was ultralight. He could make a bottle of Bud last an hour. More, even. The second bottle was always warm by the time he got to it, but he didn't mind, nor did he drink it any faster than he'd drunk the first one. What was the rush?

Two beers was enough. All it did was give him a little buzz, and when the second beer was gone he'd turn off the TV and sit at the window, smoking one cigarette after another, looking out at the city.

Then he'd go to bed. Then he'd get up and do it all over again.

The only problem was walking home.

And even that was no problem at first. He'd leave his rooming house around three in the afternoon. The diner was ten minutes away, and that left him time to eat before his shift started. Then he'd leave sometime between midnight and twelve-thirty—the guy who relieved him, a manic Albanian, had a habit of showing up ten to fifteen minutes late. Paul would retrace his earlier route, walking the seven blocks down Eighth Avenue to Sixteenth Street with a stop at the deli for cigarettes and beer.

The Rose of Singapore was the problem.

The first time he walked past the place, he didn't even notice it. By day it was just another seedy bar, but at night the neon glowed and the jukebox music poured out the door, along with the smell of spilled drinks and stale beer and something more, something unnameable, something elusive.

"If you don't want to slip," they'd told him, "stay out of slippery places."

He quickened his pace and walked on by.

The next afternoon the Rose of Singapore didn't carry the same feeling of danger. Not that he'd risk crossing the threshold, not at any hour of the day or night. He wasn't stupid. But it didn't lure him, and consequently it didn't make him uncomfortable.

Coming home was a different story.

He was thinking about it during his last hour on the job, and by the time he reached it he was walking all the way over at the edge of the sidewalk, as far from the building's entrance as he could get without stepping down into the street. He was like an acrophobe edging along a precipitous path, scared to look down, afraid of losing his balance and falling accidentally, afraid too of the impulse that might lead him to plunge purposefully into the void.

He kept walking, eyes forward, heart racing. Once he was past it he felt himself calming down, and he bought his two bottles of beer and his pack of cigarettes and went on home.

He'd get used to it, he told himself. It would get easier with time.

But, surprisingly enough, it didn't. Instead it got worse, but gradually, imperceptibly, and he learned to accommodate it. For one thing, he steered clear of the west side of Eighth Avenue, where the Rose of Singapore stood. Going to work and coming home, he kept to the opposite side of the street.

Even so, he found himself hugging the inner edge of the sidewalk, as if every inch closer to the street would put him that much closer to crossing it and being drawn mothlike into the tavern's neon flame. And, approaching the Rose of Singapore's block, he'd slow down or speed up his pace so that the traffic signal would allow him to cross the street as soon as he reached the corner. As if otherwise, stranded there, he might cross in the other direction instead, across Eighth Avenue and on into the Rose.

He knew it was ridiculous but he couldn't change the way it felt. When it didn't get better he found a way around it.

He took Seventh Avenue instead.

He did that on the weekends anyway because it was the shortest route. But during the week it added two long crosstown blocks to his pedestrian commute, four blocks a day, twenty blocks a week. That came to about three miles a week, maybe a hundred and fifty extra miles a year.

On good days he told himself he was lucky to be getting the exercise, that the extra blocks would help him stay in shape. On bad days he felt like an idiot, crippled by fear.

Then the Albanian got fired.

He was never clear on what happened. One waitress said the Albanian had popped off at the manager one time too many, and maybe that was what happened. All he knew was that one night his relief man was not the usual wild-eyed fellow with the droopy mustache but a stocky dude with a calculating air about him. His name was Dooley, and Paul made him at a glance as a man who'd done time. You could tell, but of course he didn't say anything, didn't drop any hints. And neither did Dooley.

But the night came when Dooley showed up, tied his apron, rolled up his sleeves, and said, "Give her my love, huh?" And, when Paul looked at him in puzzlement, he added, "Your girlfriend."

"Haven't got one," he said.

"You live on Eighth Avenue, right? That's what you told me. Eighth and Sixteenth, right? Yet every time you leave here you head over toward Seventh. Every single time."

"I like the exercise," he said.

"Exercise," Dooley said, and grinned. "Good word for it."

He let it go, but the next night Dooley made a similar comment. "I need to unwind when I come off work," Paul told him. "Sometimes I'll walk clear over to Sixth Avenue before I head downtown. Or even Fifth."

"That's nice," Dooley said. "Just do me a favor, will you? Ask her if she's got a sister."

"It's cold and it looks like rain," Paul said. "I'll be walking home on Eighth Avenue tonight, in case you're keeping track."

And when he left he did walk down Eighth Avenue—for one block. Then he cut over to Seventh and took what had become his usual route.

He began doing that all the time, and whenever he headed east on Twenty-second Street he found himself wondering why he'd let Dooley have such power over him. For that matter, how could he have let a seedy gin joint make him walk out of his way to the tune of a hundred and fifty miles a year?

He was supposed to be keeping it simple. Was this keeping it simple? Making up elaborate lies to explain the way he walked home? And walking extra blocks every night for fear that the Devil would reach out and drag him into a neon-lit Hell?

Then came a night when it rained, and he walked all the way home on Eighth Avenue.

It was always a problem when it rained. Going to work he could catch a bus, although he it wasn't terribly convenient. But coming home he didn't have the option, because traffic was one-way the wrong way.

So he walked home on Eighth Avenue, and he didn't turn left at Twenty-second Street, and didn't fall apart when he drew even with the Rose of Singapore. He breezed on by, bought his beer and cigarettes at the deli, and went home to watch television. But he turned the set off again after a few minutes and spent the hours until bedtime at the window, looking out at the rain, nursing the beers, smoking the cigarettes, and thinking long thoughts.

The next two nights were clear and mild, but he chose Eighth Avenue anyway. He wasn't uneasy, not going to work, not coming home, either. Then came the weekend, and then on Monday he took Eighth again, and this time on the way home he found himself on the west side of the street, the same side as the bar.

The door was open. Music, strident and bluesy, poured through it, along with all the sounds and smells you'd expect.

He walked right on by.

You're over it, he thought. He went home and didn't even turn on the TV, just sat and smoked and sipped his two longneck bottles of Bud.

Same story Tuesday, same story Wednesday.

Thursday night, steps from the tavern's open door, he thought, Why drag this out?

He walked in, found a stool at the bar. "Double scotch," he told the barmaid. "Straight up, beer chaser."

He'd tossed off the shot and was working on the beer when a woman slid onto the stool beside him. She put a cigarette between bright red lips, and he scratched a match and lit it for her.

Their eyes met, and he felt something click.

She lived over on Ninth and Seventeenth, on the third floor of a brownstone across the street from the projects. She said her name was Tiffany, and maybe it was. Her apartment was three little rooms. They sat on the couch in the front room and he kissed her a few times and got a little dizzy from it. He excused himself and went to the bathroom and looked at himself in the mirror over the sink.

You could go home now, he told the mirror image. Tell her anything, like you got a headache, you got malaria, you're really a Catholic priest or gay or both. Anything. Doesn't matter what you say or if she believes you. You could go home.

He looked into his own eyes in the mirror and knew it wasn't true.

Because he was stuck, he was committed, he was down for it. Had been from the moment he walked into the bar. No, longer than that. From the first rainy night when he walked home on Eighth Avenue. Or maybe before, maybe ever since Dooley's insinuation had led him to change his route.

And maybe it went back further than that. Maybe he was locked in from the jump, from the day they opened the gates and put him on the street. Hell, from the day he was born, even.

"Paul?"

"Just a minute," he said.

And he slipped into the kitchen. In for a penny, in for a pound, he thought, and he started opening drawers, looking for the one where she kept the knives.

A NEW DAY IN THE REAL WORLD
BY KOFI FOSU FORSON

My new day in the real world began when my bro and I hopped a cab on our way uptown. I'd been eating shit from my family for thirty years. I don't know what you want to call it—that I was born fucked up or along the way the screws in my head went loose.

I've been hospitalized. Done therapy for as long as I can remember; left high school not having lost my virginity.

Mother was and still is the most important woman I know. Some assholes looked at us back in the day and were dumb enough to think we were a married couple. It didn't help that I had my hand on her lap.

"Family." Not that "F" word. I've been pissed on shat upon damn near taken a bullet to the head all because I was the first born of a mother who gave birth to twins. You know what they say about mothers who give birth to twins. They would pull a truck with their bare hands to save a child. Well as to be expected my brothers came first. All the beating I took was for them. Here I was—the last of mother's sons to leave home.

I walked out the door without even saying a word to moms. Not sure if she was even looking at me as I walked out that door. I had to get out. It was killing me. I wasn't a kid no more. But there I was every morning sitting with her to tea just like I used to as a boy. Damn I might as well have been sucking her nipple. That's what her friends would say when they walked in, these fucking women friends of hers would look at her. "Ain't he done sucking those tits of yours." I'd walk into the bedroom flip through porn magazines to get the thought of mother's breasts away from me.

My bro and me were sitting in the back of a livery cab. I was stone cold done. It seemed like I had no life in me. He sat there keeping me company. Somehow I think he knew what was going through my mind.

The car was speeding up the highway. New York City skyline passing us by. It was a beautiful day. The sun was out. There were no clouds around. They were all gone except the color blue. In my heart I was aching. My eyes fell to my feet. Complete silence inside that cab.

My bro and I were not close but living together all those years. He had a good idea what I had been through. Those nights when he would go out clubbing and I would stay home. He would bring back a girl, bang her while I was in the other room. I would hear them going at it. I'd be lying there listening. Sometimes I felt like touching myself. I never did but I felt like shit.

Depression was my thing. I was not schizophrenic or psycho. That summer when I got out of high school I didn't go out. I stayed home for weeks. I went and told mama I was losing my mind. She said they couldn't help me because they didn't believe in doctors. That was it. She walked away from me and that was it. I survived that night though I held a knife to my wrist.

The following morning I went and talked to the family priest. He gave me some advice.

He sat there looking at me. "What could possibly be wrong with you?" I had to tell him I had been suffering from depression all this time and it was kicking my ass. I needed a way out. Pretty soon thereafter he got me a social worker and here we are: I'm on my way to my new apartment.

The car moseyed on up to the sidewalk of the building. My bro and I got out with my shit, made our way up the stairs and into my new apartment. The roommate was waiting: a tall as shit skinny motherfucker. He had eyes like an owl. I could tell he'd been smoking up.

This wasn't like home. There was a lot of tension between me and this guy. He was intimidating. I suffered from an emotional disease but I carried myself as normal as possible. It was clear to me the man sitting before me had a problem. He looked disturbed like he had been in the woods for a while. He smelled that funk of a smell which came from a man who hadn't showered for days. But in my own little way I had heart. I embraced him as an older brother, uncle or whatever.

That night I got to know him a bit better we sat drinking beers. He told me all about himself. How he came from the south and had been homeless for a long time. Pandhandling was not his thing but he collected soda cans to make a few dollars. He loved smoking up sometimes about five times a day.

So as I was walking to the fridge to get another beer I asked him . . . I had the nerve to ask him if he was a drug addict. There was silence at first so I asked him again. "Are you addicted to drugs?" He stood up—all six feet six of him—and he put his hands together made that sign that says fuck you but he did it like he meant it and shouted, "FUCK YOU!"

He walked by me—waddling, not walking, but waddling intense as a coked-up motherfucker. I swear I thought
he was gonna fuck me up right there, like, tear into me—
make minced meat outtta this downtown boy that I was.

He entered the shower. I could hear the water running
he was yelling insults at me. He was pissed off. I didn't
know what I had done wrong. He kept yelling.

"WHO THE FUCK ARE YOU? I BREAK PEOPLE!
YOUR KIND MOTHERFUCKER!

I ran into my room took my shirt off. I was scared as
shit. Never imagined it would come to this . . . trapped
inside a room, not wanting to leave, not knowing if I could.
But I stayed in that room afraid for my life. Somehow
I didn't think he would kill me although I knew he could.
I told myself if this is it come and get me. Come and get
me. I'm ready. Come and get me.

THE PRESENTATION
BY PEDRO PONCE

He had been warned about the City. The City was alive, he was told, its streets swelling with breath, its bridges and towers sounding the air like ravenous antennae. He had lived all his life in its shadow, whether walking to school against its distant skyline, or dreaming of living there once he had grown older. But he had never left his native town. He was a competent worker, already promoted once; the fact that he was being entrusted with business in the City was a sure sign that he had a long future ahead with the Company. He was getting good at the business, but he could not claim the passion of those in management, or those marked early on as management material. He set these thoughts aside now as he made the necessary calls to reserve his train and hotel.

At street level, he heard a voice call behind him. "Need ride?"

He turned to see a sallow-faced man reaching for one of his bags. "I'm waiting for someone," he replied, pulling the bag away.

The stranger was insistent. "No problem. I take. I take."

From the periphery of his growing panic, he heard a

woman's voice. "Is there a problem?" she said. She positioned herself between them. "I'll take it from here, thank you." He followed her out to the Company car.

Their conversation was frequently stilted by the driver's acceleration into the nearest open lane. As they waited for the traffic lights to change, a crew of workers in dark jumpsuits probed a tangle of tubes springing up through a hole in the sidewalk. The car began to fill with a dank, fecal smell.

"How long have you worked for the Company?" he asked.

"Three years. But I don't see myself staying much longer."

"What will you do instead?"

"I don't know. I model part-time. I have a show tomorrow night. You should come." The liaison handed him a black and white flyer. A woman clutched both sides of her face mid-scream, her mouth tearing a black seam into the pallor of her features. She was fringed above by dripping letters: CRIMES OF FASHION.

His hotel appeared beyond the tinted glass. Its windows stretched the length of the entire block.

He stayed in, ordering room service and going over his presentation one more time. He was in bed by ten-thirty, hoping to get to the office by seven-forty-five. He tossed restlessly for half an hour before resigning himself to sleeplessness and whatever was on television.

He paused at a wide shot of his hotel. He thought he recognized the same bellman that had taken his bags after the liaison dropped him off.

A woman in a burgundy skirt and blazer said welcome in English, while her words were translated into other languages at the top and bottom of the screen. She wished the viewer a safe and happy stay. He began to nod off as the woman explained the icons for laundry, room service and other amenities. In profile, a hotel guest could be seen sleeping soundly to the reassuring voice of the woman in burgundy. He adjusted his pillow in order to see the screen more clearly. The sleeper curled more deeply onto the pillow. He raised a fist to rub at a sudden itch in his eye. The sleeper's arm reached blindly into the darkness. The woman's voice grew louder; he could feel it bristling through his limbs.

He sat up. The television was off. He watched himself breathing in the dimness of the screen.

He arrived right at eight. The liaison from the previous day led him to a large conference room that looked out on the City's northern skyline.

He felt a tap on his shoulder. Turning quickly, his nose nearly brushed a pale hand offered stiffly in greeting. It belonged to a wiry man in a striped charcoal suit. "Sorry," the man said. "I was in Processing for years. Bad for the eyes. First time in the City?"

"Yes," he replied, unzipping his briefcase and withdrawing his notes and projector. "Very impressive."

The man took one of the seats opposite and folded his hands together. The stripes on his lapel indicated management level. "The City can be quite overwhelming one's first time."

"Oh, it is. In a good way."

The Manager grinned. "Yes. At any rate, welcome. We are eager to hear your report."

His recall, by this point, was automatic. He withdrew his collapsible pointer and approached the screen, listening to the clicks as he opened the pointer. The clicks were muted by his own voice reciting percentages and invoice numbers, and the percussion of a pneumatic drill outside. The further he went, the more he felt pinned by the conference table against the span of windows at his back. The glare of the track lights intensified, until his audience all but vanished into the walls behind it.

The Manager was applauding. "Well done," he said. The liaison jotted something down on her wireless tablet without looking up.

The Manager excused himself. Before he left, he handed over a small business envelope. "Enjoy yourself on us tonight." The Manager fished briefly with both hands for a firm congratulatory shake.

The liaison stayed behind as he packed up his things. "Everyone's a bit nervous presenting the first time," she said.

He looked at her. "I thought it went pretty well."

"Of course," said the liaison.

When he reached the lobby, he checked his watch. It was nine-thirteen. The sun was blanching the storefronts outside. He squeezed into the narrowing berth of a revolving door and emerged into a blinding wind that cut through his clothes. He followed the map provided earlier by the concierge back to his hotel.

***

He awoke at five in the afternoon to the digital chirp of his room phone. He fumbled the receiver to his ear.

"Will you be needing our cleaning staff today?"

"No," he answered. The automated message continued to describe the menu of options. When he had pressed the number for no service, the voice wished him a good evening.

The Manager's envelope contained a sheaf of restaurant recommendations, an expense card, and a ticket to something called *The Presentation*. Several of the restaurant flyers featured ads describing it as "the theater experience of the season." A picture showed the small cast mid-performance, one actor pointing in accusation, another looking aside, in the direction of the audience. He had enough time before the show to walk towards the Theater District and find somewhere to eat.

The play, for the most part, consisted of obscenities repeated in various cadences. The obscenities were polysyllabic at comedic points in the narrative, turning monosyllabic when the story took a more serious turn. The central characters were a man and a woman who shared a mysterious past. The man had come back to reclaim something, something the woman kept in a rectangular tin she would open and contemplate during each of her soliloquies. Near the close of the first act, the man interrupted a bitter exchange with a request to use the woman's bathroom.

"Isn't that how it always is," the woman said as the man stormed into the wings, "retreating to tend that sad swollen sac. Fuck," she said softly, reaching for her tin.

He suddenly felt the fullness of his own bladder. He navigated the dark between sections and left the auditorium. Squinting at the lobby's sudden light, he stumbled in the direction of the lavatories. The men's room was narrow and overheated and beneath the sting of antibacterial soap, he smelled the sulfurous air from yesterday's car ride.

At the dappled marble sink, he recognized the actor who had just left the stage. He had laid aside his fedora and was smoothing the unruly strands of his comb-over. Close up, the actor's makeup gave his features a vivid, watery look.

"Great work," he said to the actor, who ran his hands under the soap dispenser. The actor ignored him, buttoning up his coat before leaving the lavatory.

He followed shortly after and was about to open the auditorium door when he was stopped by one of the ushers. The usher pointed to the words over the central entrance:

FOR THE ENJOYMENT OF OTHERS

AND OUR FINE ENSEMBLE

PATRONS NOT READMITTED

UNTIL NEXT INTERMISSION

"But—" he began. An usher silenced him with a raised hand. He folded his arms and heard a crinkling in his coat pocket. Behind him, the auditorium erupted in knowing laughter. He withdrew the liaison's flyer and left to hail a cab.

***

He sat through a procession of gaunt figures displaying clothes cut from the same palette of pearl, charcoal, scarlet, and mist. The models entered from beneath an enormous banner on which the word EVASION appeared in enormous fading type. Small cameras were mounted along the walkway at various levels, projecting images on three screens simultaneously. The images had the stark, grainy look of surveillance footage; the date and time appeared at the bottom of each screen. He found the liaison framed by Camera Two, her face pressed to the runway between forked heels. Her eyes and mouth were open; a dark streak dribbled from her lips. He looked down from the screen and found her among the bodies outlined in chalk marking the models' path.

He was surprised when she found him after the show. She had yet to change out of her stage clothes. The fake blood on her face had dried into powdery crust. "Can you do me a favor?" she asked. She handed him a wallet camera. "I wanted some pictures before I get completely out of character. Corpses are going to be big this year." She led him into a changing room and lay flat at his feet. Her blouse rose to reveal the smoothness of her belly.

She laughed, her cheeks vivid against the bare floor. "Stop," she said.

"What?"

"You're making me—" Her torso swelled with breath. "OK," she announced. She tensed for a moment, then went completely limp. Her blush vanished. Her skin seemed to absorb the gray hue of the dressing room walls. He aimed and shot.

There was a knock at the door. The doorway was blocked by a tall figure that still looked dressed for the runway.

"We still going out?" A woman's voice.

"Yeah," the liaison said, eagerly. She stood up. "This is—" He introduced himself.

The model looked him up and down. "We better hurry before Curfew."

"You should come with us!" the liaison said. "It's your last night."

Her friend's lips were silver. They barely flinched as he agreed to join them.

***

They were still blocks from their destination when the liaison's friend slowed her steps and began digging through her purse. The liaison bounced excitedly as she accepted one white capsule and a small plastic cup. "A pick-me-up," her friend said. "You have to special order weeks in advance." She said this vaguely in his direction.

The liaison popped the capsule without a word to either of them. Her eyes and mouth closed with a satisfied expression before she resumed walking. She kept the cup palmed in her right hand.

They crossed an avenue and continued east. Under the orange streetlights, the liaison began shuffling rhythmically. They turned a corner and in the distance, he could hear the pulse of music, its rhythm matching the liaison's perfectly. At a stalled crosswalk, she pulled his arms around her and swayed against him. He felt the coldness of her earlobe at his mouth.

The light changed and the liaison bounded to the next corner. When he reached the other side, he saw she was staring into her empty cup. Her mouth closed abruptly and her face arranged itself into a smooth blank. She dipped her chin delicately over the cup and expelled a thin stream of orange fluid. Her friend's spasms were more intense. Orange beads formed along the sides as she filled the cup with her retching. She gulped the frothy contents before they could spill to the street. She sopped with her tongue at drops that stained her fingers.

A long line snaked around the corner opposite. At the visible end, people waited for entrance into a rosy corridor surmounted by letters that filled and refilled with liquid light: DREAMHOUSE. The music inside was drowned out by a police patrol marking the hour before Curfew. On the sides of the black van, a narrow screen displayed the current Threat Level. The liaison danced defiantly into the passing din; several booed or hoisted middle fingers. He turned to find the bouncer gesturing to him impatiently, the blue velvet barrier inches from being reclasped.

He emerged alone into a slightly larger room. The color of the walls changed at regular intervals from deep red to deep blue. The source was a scale model of the building he had just entered. Small plastic figures trailed nearly completely around the perimeter. Part of the wall ahead seemed to sink into a doorway, but it was solid when he approached. He turned again to the miniature building. The lights continued to dim and saturate the room. He thought he saw movement when he heard a voice.

"Sir?"

The speaker was dressed in a dark suit with no tie, rendering his figure a muscular ellipse.

"Excuse me, sir?" the speaker repeated flatly. "Can you read?"

He nodded.

"Then I'm sure you can understand." The speaker indicated a placard screwed into the wall nearby.

GET DOWN OR GET OUT

The bell of a hand lantern slid from his coat sleeve. The lantern had a thick handle that took some time before the speaker's fist clenched the end.

***

Outside, the wind intensified, carrying the night's last noises. He pushed against it, searching for a cab.

The street narrowed between lengths of chain link. Arrows marked a detour around the latest construction. The plywood path tilted loosely as he walked.

He followed irregularly spaced bulbs down the corridor, where shadows moved at an approaching turn. He joined the back of a line waiting under a cavernous arch-way. The line snaked far ahead before rising over a wide flight of steps. The steps led to a platform in the distance where figures waited, occasionally looking over the edge into a pit that extended parallel into the visible distance at either side.

From his place on the platform, he saw a second plat-form rising opposite. The faces there were indistinct. He pushed his way to the front. He craned his neck for a better view. A figure on the opposite platform matched his move-ments. The features edged by the dimness overhead were his own.

The figure's face was lost now among seated silhou-ettes. On his own side, the gathering crowd shifted more tightly around him, edging him forward. He waited. At any moment, the face would reemerge, streaked in orange light. He would be looking. And he would know.

ZEN AND THE ART OF HOOKING
BY RONALD H. BASS

Mimosa O'Toole, seated in front of her old ThinkPad, yawned as she realized there was nothing more to transcribe. She logged onto kexp.org and began sipping from an oversized mug of espresso on the tray table to her left. Opening up her teacher's autobiography at the beginning, waves of desire washed over her as she read for perhaps the thousandth time, *"Becoming an enlightened master was so blissfully easy that for the first couple of weeks I actually half-doubted I had become one. Here's how it happened: Marie-Louise picked me up while I was having country sausage for lunch at au Babylone and took me back to her six room flat on rue de Varennes, just up the street from where Edith Wharton used to live. After a couple of glasses of Calvados she fucked my brains out in all sorts of imaginative ways for the remainder of the afternoon and evening. As the sun was just about to come up, she whispered a mantra in my ear and made me repeat it 108 times. Afterwards, laughing mirthfully, she announced, 'Voila! You are now Yogi Baksheesh, Spiritual Advisor to the Exceptionally Evolved.' And so I was."*

Closing the book, Mimosa recalled the words Yogi Baksheesh said to her as she was leaving his studio two nights ago, "When I was twelve, my grandfather Friedrich, an astrophysicist, who was on his deathbed, said to me, 'We change universes far more often than a reasonably hygienic person changes underwear. The problem, if indeed it is such, is that very few of us have even the faintest notion, except perhaps in dreams, that this is occurring.'" Snapping out of her reverie Mimosa reminded herself, "And now it's time to go to the gym."

Later, while walking to her office from the Crunch on Lafayette Street, Mimosa wanted to run through the upcoming workday but instead she initially found herself focusing on another one of the exercises she learned from Yogi Baksheesh. Mimosa had a hard time at first with this meditation technique, but eventually it became so effective as to become almost addicting. The first step was to sit or lie comfortably and to get sexually aroused any way she wanted to. Then she was to start masturbating, but she was never to allow herself to have a complete, earth-shaking orgasm. To whatever extent possible she was supposed to keep herself from getting wet and especially to avoid ejaculating. The goal was to reach for fainter and fainter orgasms that paradoxically were more and more powerful, and in their own peculiar way earth shattering (rather than merely earth-shaking). The point of the exercise, according to Yogi Baksheesh, was for Mimosa to free herself from the constraints imposed by birth onto this planet and to begin visiting some of the quirkier realms of a five-dimensional universe. To accomplish this she was to imagine a current of electric energy flowing down her legs, through the ground, and into the molten core of the earth. Then she was to imagine this energy flowing back up through the ground and up through her feet and legs until it reached her root chakra where she was to imagine a bright red sphere turning clockwise, and then up through the second chakra in her genital area with an orange sphere turning clockwise, and similarly up through the other six chakras with their associated colors, and finally as a spray of energy cascading out of the top of her head and traveling to the furthest point of the universe. Then she was to reverse this process and pull the energy back down into her body, first into the chakra at the top of her head with a sphere of violet light, now turning counterclockwise, and from there into the middle of her forehead with an indigo sphere turning counterclockwise, and down through the other six chakras, and finally down through her legs and feet. At the end of the meditation she was to deposit this energy back into the molten core at the center of the earth.

Mimosa was discovering the intensity of this exercise to be increasing exponentially over time. And she acknowledged with a silent nod the inevitability of Bronc White being the most frequent mute witness to her moments of boundless ecstasy. It was strange to associate the word "mute" with Bronc, who was the polar opposite of mute in every conceivable way. But poor Bronc, Mimosa's one-and-only for the two years they were together (although she harbored doubts about whether she was his one-and-only) was dead, murdered by a fiend who was yet to be apprehended.

With a shudder she recalled the front-page article that appeared in the *New York Post*, the day after the murder that described how his corpse was discovered in the basement men's room of Bowery Poetry Club with a vintage ice pick lodged in the back of his skull. There was a large sign that looked like the front of a sandwich board hung around his neck. On it was written: HOTSKY, TOTSKY, NO MORE TROTSKY. And it was signed in red, in what turned out to be Bronc's own blood: THE LILLIAN HELLMAN

BRIGADES. Bronc had just given the final reading of his career, in which he enraged a large portion of the reflexively left-wing audience with incendiary new poems such as *Epitaph for Allen Ginsberg*: "He saw the best behinds/Of his generation/Destroyed by hemorrhoids."

Thinking about this meditation exercise also brought back memories from her student days when she was working in a New Age massage parlor to pay her tuition and living expenses while she was a student at FIT. Mimosa had no financial support from her family. She was conceived after a brunch during which her mother drank five mimosas, which was coincidentally the last time her mother ever saw her father.

Mimosa never once stopped to think that what she was doing could by the wildest stretch of the imagination be considered prostitution. She was just performing a health-restoring reflexology procedure. Although it was true she was manipulating dicks she always wore latex gloves. And she was vigilant about making sure that her customers never ejaculated. The primary goal was to further their quest for enlightenment although Mimosa suspected many of her clients were more interested in experiencing good vibrations than in merging with the void.

Marco struck her as more of a thrill-seeker than a devotee of esoteric knowledge, and he was perhaps the sleaziest person she had ever worked on. So it wasn't a total shock when, after she had taken one-hundred dollars in cash from him, he pulled out a badge and identified himself as Detective Marcello Villela, NYPD Vice Squad. He seemed to derive an inordinate amount of pleasure in putting her in handcuffs, but what was even weirder was that on the ride to the station house he kept asking her questions about acting technique, and quoting Jerzy Grotowski, Constantin

Stanislavski, and Sanford Meisner. He also told her in excruciating detail about his appearances on the various *Law and Order* shows filming in the city, and about his extensive wardrobe of vintage rockabilly clothing. She wasn't at all surprised to learn that he had grown up in Bensonhurst.

Looking back on this experience years later Mimosa always acknowledged her debt of gratitude to Marcello. If it hadn't been for him she would probably never have written *Zen and the Art of Hooking*, and her career might never have attained the stratospheric orbital trajectory it currently rockets around in. Still, it was more than a little creepy when Marco showed up last Friday as a customer at MackinWear. He wouldn't tell her how he got the keypad number and then he plunked down twelve-hundred dollars in cash for a purple Elizabethan-style pimp hat with an ostrich feather. He also mentioned that he had gotten a promotion and was now a homicide detective.

It seemed odd to Mimosa that Marco turned up just as she was about to liquidate the highly profitable, but dodgy—at least from a tax standpoint—MackinWear store where all sales were cash on the barrelhead. But now she was going completely legit. The Working Girl stores dispensed clothing, designed for whores and women who wanted to dress like whores, in malls from coast to coast. Although the corporate office was in midtown, she still maintained her private office in the flagship store on Ludlow Street.

It wasn't unusual for men to be shopping in Working Girl for clothes for their girlfriends or wives. This provided adequate cover for the secret door with keypad entry that could be accessed from Mimosa's private office. There was someone on duty in MackinWear even when she was out of the office. Usually it was Slim Dunkk, a six-foot-eleven, three hundred twenty five pound rapper who augmented his musical income working as a high-paid sales clerk slash security specialist. The MackinWear customer base was somewhat suspect but nobody had ever tried to fuck with Slim.

Arriving at her office Mimosa saw she had a text from Slim that read, "Q is here." Dr. Heydrich Quisslinger had arrived to negotiate the final purchase of the entire MakinWear stock. He intended to give the items away as gifts to the dictator clients of Quisslinger Associates, his global-risk consulting firm.

As Mimosa walked through the door into the MackinWear shop she heard Slim laughing and telling Dr. Quisslinger, "Heidi—you cannot charge a chinchilla coat on your American Express card."

Mimosa lit up a joint. She took a toke and handed it to Dr. Quisslinger who took a toke and tried to pass it on to Slim who shook his head and indicated that it should go back to Mimosa. After a ten-minute conversation, a high six-figure purchase price was agreed upon. Dr. Quisslinger made a call on his cell phone and three minutes later, two young Yale alums in matching grey suits arrived carrying briefcases in both hands. They placed the briefcases next to the door and left without saying a word. Slim counted the money and nodded to Mimosa who told Dr. Quisslinger he could send a van to collect the merchandise after nine that evening.

All three of them jumped as the door opened and Yogi Baksheesh walked into MackinWear. He looked around, sniffing the air very loudly.

Mimosa, collecting her wits, said, "Dr. Quisslinger, I would like you to meet my yoga teacher, Stephen von Ellinghausen. We have a lesson scheduled and MackinWear is usually so quiet that it's a good place to do it."

Yogi Baksheeh continued sniffing and said in a concerned tone of voice, "I smell a cockroach."

Dr. Quisslinger stood up to leave. He said, "Mimosa, thank you for your hospitality. Slim, please call my office if you think you are going to be on the job market. Mr. von Ellinghausen, it was a pleasure to make your acquaintance."

When the door closed Yogi Baksheesh, continuing to sniff the air volubly, walked around the store for a couple of minutes. When he sat down, he told Mimosa and Slim, "I was wrong. It was not a cockroach. It was a dung beetle. Dr. Quisslinger is going to choke to death on a piece of pernil while bending over to look up a woman's skirt in Cafecito. He will then be reborn as Hatchling #3147, the dung beetle known as Gregor Samsara."

THRUSH

BY JANE ORMEROD

Naomi eats birds, I'm telling you. Not in a strangled, all fingers at once manner, but rather with one hand behind her back, opening the door for others.

I didn't understand. My God, Naomi, I didn't understand. Foaming heart in your mouth, feathers in with your teeth, bird's head in throat, tail down, blinded. Deathly-smeared scissors by your feet. In your right fist you triumphantly held the sparrow's tongue

You were beside yourself, you told me.

I want to go back.

I first found Naomi with a bag of laundry over in Strand Book Store. She wore this baby-doll pink dress cut from the curtains she stole at Nicole's party. Well now, that poodle-tramp style grates with me sometimes and so—ignoring her protests— I pulled Naomi out of that place and we strode brazenly out onto the wet indigo street, blazing through it all, and we almost went shopping but temper temper tantrums from my baby meant noodle food so we ate instead. Together like blossom.

Some people, it is held, eat like there's no tomorrow, others eat like birds. Naomi ordered at least twice as much as she needed, then asked for a doggy bag. It was a happy Naomi that waved to the cooks and the smiling waiters, as we left the restaurant, smiling together. They were waving and smiling those cooks, waiters, the other diners. The dedicated maidens, the soon-to-be-saints. They were all dancing and waving like they were diseased. They wouldn't give up.

The carrier bag split on the way back and Naomi got noodles all over her shoes. She threw everything away, announced she'd see me tomorrow, and walked home barefoot.

Now, to get back to the birds. Naomi had started by just cutting out their tongues, keeping the birds alive but speechless, set free never to sing cheery milk songs again in cherry tree neighborhoods. She tore, teased, or sliced out the tongues, out of their trapping throats. Yes, she shaved speech with pinpoint accuracy.

"Try spreading the news now," laughed Naomi.

I'm not sure what she did with the tongues she amassed. Tiny, embarrassed things they would be. Destroying the evidence maybe seemed too large an act for such small fry, but later there were no half victims. Naomi, when you got bored with tongues you put away the scissors and aimed straight for the jugular. My little sweetened heart bleeds with the others, you know.

Naomi started sending letters to the families of the birds. Kind Naomi. Candid Naomi.

"Devilled bird dust stars," she scrawled at the top of the page.

"Dear, dear, devilled birds. Dead stars. Daddy's done what Momma couldn't, but Naomi was second and I'm faster, more ruthless, clearer and cleaner. Bye-bye, birdies. Bye-bye, treat hearts."

Magic moments from my manic Naomi. She was my treasure. Let's hear more.

"Why must I sit here and watch you regurgitate? Die, die, die. Cannot know. Cannot need. Do not resent me, just try to resist me."

I could not resist her.

Naomi social-danced on a Wednesday at the i Bar and Lounge on Church. She'd got the sly, two-tone shuffle backwards and, yes, the boys would die for one of her soft focus smiles as she backslid round the cracked basement floor. That night, as I watched her dance with the boys, I imagined Naomi as a young racehorse. Iron on her feet, iron in mouth, on back, on saddle, in weights. A short-skirted horse skater, round and round and round and round, circling those Aqueduct boys. Look! Naomi's head has a luscious smile, she has a luxury tail. Her forelegs wave at the crowd. She's a laughing hyena in this meat market, fish tank, Great Dane statue, paddock . . .

Don't choose a racehorse by name alone. Examine its mouth. See those tombstone teeth, that suckling tongue. Grass-stained teeth. Breath that smells like fields. Don't worry boys, she might not bite.

"Phone me, Naomi," I said, as we parted for the third time that evening.

"Yeah, yeah, yeah," and she was off with a bulge in her handbag.

Love it, girl. Love your breakdown spine, and your back-down smile, and your backoff stance, and your Berkoff language. That way you have of inhaling my sentences. And your breath was my downfall, my nightmare, my hearse. For three weeks I carried the treason you taught me, the treason you whispered to me, for the love that was promised me. For three weeks I couldn't breathe without you, couldn't live without you, and for three weeks you teased me with letters until the morning of the splashed bloodbath.

No more tongues. It chokes, the feathers down your throat. The small gasping cries, the tickle, the sharpness of the beak, the pounding wings, pulsating breath from the red breast, warm underbelly. The eye that suddenly glazes: vacant. Then the first trickle, the ringed legs, of the blood, and the death rattle that seems never-ending and the barbs and claws and green nasal sounds.

It's the scratch not the itch that alerts me. It's the intermittent mark down your left cheek. Naomi. You stuttered turkey and it was all over.

Naomi garbaged and gourmeted her way out of adversity and into complicity, thanking the Lord for East Village feathers on the way. Naomi looks so sweet, looks so good when she is grateful. Yes, if it wasn't for that birdbrain slave anklet, I'd have believed her fully.

In the end I didn't beat out the bushes with the business of the birds and I took it to the press and police. Yet the feeling of release and the flurry of excitement worried me.

"Ruffling the feathers of the establishment!" one paper said, although others called her "a menace, a murderous witch, a brainless bitch, a dangerous precedent, an alarming influence."

"Headlines that hurt!" cried Naomi, but deadlines moved closer and I saw Naomi suffer when the evidence was called, as tongues wagged, and she became tied into a corner.

Someone saw a crow and named it an omen.

The judge called order and proclaimed it a decoy.

And the defence shouted, "Irony!" and explained about nature, and supply and demand.

The courtroom hushed as Naomi calmly told how the entrails were my youth, the ribcage was her influence, and the beak would always be my reference. And she sits there in her *Fuck You Sparrow* tee shirt and she shimmers.

I try to remember if I was ever like Naomi, if I was ever that young. If I ever felt that golden idealism which was her talisman against people like me. You know, however much she needs me now, I'm not convinced Naomi even liked me that much. I wanted her to find me interesting, funny, all those sorts of New York things. I wanted to make her laugh out loud. When she smiled, I sometimes cried . . . she was so wonderful. I wanted her to put her arms around me. I wanted to feel her shoulder blades tighten and her shoulder to dampen. I wanted to be like her and I couldn't.

Younger, taller, thinner. Tiny, stolen, silver sandals. I could never be her.

I try to imagine I am. It's possible. I might be misleading you, deliberately deceiving you. Leading you on, pulling you into quandaries with me. Come on, place your feet in this trap. Artists, I think it is said by some, are supposed to hold up a mirror to the world. This image I paint of Naomi, is it a reflection of myself?

I could be my Naomi. I am doubled at once in size. At this moment I could be her, not with her, but I could be my baby. Everything would be instantaneous. Spontaneous . . . almost. I would be rapid, I would be monstrous. I am a huge Naomi. Now I have weapons, now I have new teeth, now I have dead blood. Now I am a natural. Stay with me. Stay here with me.

It's a nice idea, I think. Sometimes I fancy reinventing

myself, but it's not true. Not now. I can't be in two places and I've kind of got used to myself, so no. Believe me. Naomi is real. It's not me eating the thrushes and, whatever Naomi claims, the entrails were never ever my youth. Naomi ran away, not before she was found out, not before anything could be done, but before she could be punished. Before she could say goodbye.

A while ago now I went to the cinema, Union Square, sometime in the summer it must have been. Three girls sat in front of me. As I grow older I find it harder and harder to tell people's ages but I knew, from their birthday chatter, these girls were fourteen. Anyway, they started discussing what their ideal age was, and they decided it would be eighteen. They wanted to spend their lives being between eighteen and nineteen. Soon as they reached nineteen, they'd spring back to eighteen again. And they chose this golden age immediately. One said *seventeen, no, no, eighteen*, and the others said *yes, eighteen. Eighteen all our glorious lives.*

You know, they didn't need to explain the reasons to one another. They didn't say why not twenty, or twenty-three, or nineteen, or seventeen? From their four years in waiting, they knew. Unanimously. Without speaking. Together they would be eighteen. This was it. They could see eighteen shining in the distance and they were the bridesmaids. And, as the film started, the three girls squealed at their first sight of male muscle, and I thought I am twenty years older than your ideal age. I am almost a quarter of a century older than you are now, and I grew older and older over the next two hours. I aged more rapidly than those three impatient girls.

I can't remember. I can't understand. I just cannot make sense of it. No.

What I'm trying to figure is . . . did Naomi keep any secrets? If she allowed me to visit, paraded her collection of tongues, then granted me access to the terrifying vision of her scrambling bird bones and cramming bird heads into her mouth . . . well, what other despairing pleasures did she conceal? Did she think I was not worthy of?

Do you remember I told you about the noodles? How my sweet girl chucked away her shoes once they were covered in the takeout juices? Immediately after this accident, she ordered me away, although earlier she'd invited me home. Watching her leave, I saw her walk along a strip of new tarmac. She left soft impressions behind like gentle kisses. A softness, I think, she otherwise did not possess. My Naomi was flimsy, fragile. Flirtatious of course, but also worldly: aware of the destruction she could cause. Sly in those shoes and fast in that skirt, I hated her for the generalizations she carried. In her wallet I found a photo of an ambulance.

I was too scared even to retrieve the shoes from the curb. Maybe I was looking for curses even then. Trying to remove myself from her, not wanting anything to stick on me, something to come home with me.

It was like owning a dead man's coat. I felt worried death might become aware of my existence, as if death could remain behind. Rubbed off. Like death was a perfume. Sitting in a thrift store, watching quietly, waiting for new customers to smear itself onto.

My instincts were whispering *do not go near Naomi smelling of death*. If you buy a dead man's coat, clean it. Put in life with your dry-cleaning fluids. Replace the lining, a buttonhole even. Wear a hat with it— if death cannot see your face clearly you may be saved. Garlic is for vampires only but a wooden stake is always good for protection.

Birds do not carry stakes though they might well have need of them. They own one coat only and can be caught with a butterfly net by children. Some do not fly despite having wings. The highest bird is lower than a pilot, and the earth is small and easy to navigate. Budgerigars have now left Australia and may be found in small cages, often conveniently situated near open windows where a confident thief can, with one hand, unlock the door and, with the other, swaddle the bird, squeezing out life, teasing with freedom, and then swallowing with gusto.

Parakeets and lovebirds are similar. Parrots more of a challenge for the novice and, if allowed to escape, will talk. Sparrows are your everyday meat and potatoes, as are pigeons. Seagulls reside both at the seaside and on landfills. As they have no taste, they are not for the discerning. Larks are sublime, eagles inspiring, and blackbirds are fit for a king.

Yes, some birds are songbirds and they're always tasty. Bluebirds are pretty but dull. Puffins are sweet, vultures are sour, an albatross a burden to get home . . .

And now they have disappeared and now they are dead. The plumage attracted Naomi. The twitching nervousness tuning into the smell of mortality that accompanies it. Such a knowing mortality. No despair, nor any hope.

What did Naomi smell of?

She smelt like Dennis Hopper. She smelt of things I couldn't realize, of things I missed out on, of things that would never happen to me. She smelt of huge loss yet huge temptation. She smelt of expectations, cat sick, catgut, mountain ranges, Mexican treasures. Drownings. Failing lungs and falling temperatures at night. Scented elbows from leaning on the New York edge.

I could smell the desperation on her eyelids.

She looked enchanted but acted seasick as she lurched from crisis to crisis to pleasure. She smelt of dying fishermen, of improbable whales, multiplicity and nightingale floors.

It's the nightingale floor which will trap you, Naomi. Tiny triggers randomly jointed in that corridor you will eventually find. Planks to lose you your head before you reach my room. Your feet will betray you, joists will sing out treacherously. Already I hear them and so, I think, can you. I am surrounded by my nightingale floor; my engineering will clock your sweet calls. It is random, unbeatable, and I am safe. I have a nightingale floor as a mattress and it does not soften sound but amplifies, fills to my rafters, and I shall know.

I am asleep on the blackened floor and I am sliding, tilting my horizon. Holding the roughened blanket over, around my features, I am disappearing again, going under. I am dying on the floor. The floor is getting softer and I am shrinking into myself. Now arms, legs too, are folding. I am turning in the gloom, turning. I am a rock, a shrinking boulder, smoother, smaller. No arms, no legs, still sliding. Cushioned by all that I know. Alone on the nightingale floor. Tiny, tiny, getting smaller. Leaving the city, smelling the bracken, hawthorn and aging woods.

Nearly there now.

The feathers are in your stomach and your bones are in my teeth.

Do, Naomi. Do Do Do Do Do.

BENCHES

BY PETER D. MARRA

Morning:

One subway bench was tipped forward, chained to the other bench by its side. Both benches were bound together with yellow police tape, bound and gagged lying together on the platform.

About 50 feet away, clothed in the sickly fluorescent light, an elderly Asian man was playing an erhu. People milled around on the platform. Sirens could be heard through the grating, mixing with his music.

Max was walking up and down the platform. His only purpose was to wait for the train. That and to finish the *New York Times* crossword puzzle. He walked, and then stopped occasionally, trying to complete the puzzle.

The announcements of train arrivals cut through and merged with the existing noise every 30 seconds or so. The resulting din bounced inside Max's head. The combination of screechy erhu, sirens, random people, chatter, and MTA announcements was building inside his brain, deep in the lobes . . . a dull hum growing larger.

He pressed harder with his pen into the crossword until he was shredding the paper. He stared at the crossword's thin gash and reluctantly threw it into the trash receptacle on the platform.

"It's not perfect anymore. Try again tomorrow morning," he thought.

Svelte hip young things were also on the platform coolly staring at their feet . . . Slowly admiring their new shoes and boots, checking each other out.

The Asian guy's music was going faster now. Max recognized the tune—"Pachelbel's Canon"—only now it was strident and irritating.

"It's only six-thirty in the morning."

Starting to say his morning prayers, Max realized he couldn't do it. It was too noisy and the shadows were moving too quickly. He looked down at the subway tracks. The cute rat he saw every morning was doing its morning routine of running up and down the tracks. It looked happy. One time Max thought of marking the rat with paint so he could see if it was the same rat he was seeing every morning. But as time went on he was convinced that it was the same rat: it had a particular grace of movement and a very unique smile . . . A whimsical grin.

Wanting to sit down, Max looked for a seat on the platform. The only seats were the benches in yellow caution tape bondage. He leaned against a post and started to regret throwing away his newspaper.

The newspaper with the crossword puzzle.

A week here . . . a week . . .there . . .

One more repetition . . .

And then tomorrow. . . Another repetition.

He noticed he was starting a cold sweat. He was worried that maybe he was bleeding internally.

The train arrived and he let it pass because it was crowded. He let a few more pass until one arrived on the heels of another. It always happened sooner or later: two trains would arrive in quick succession. It seemed that he was the only one who could figure this out. He had made a little project out of timing the trains: at around seven-twenty-one, one train would arrive bursting with people. It would be so crowded that the passengers would be steadying themselves by touching the ceiling of the train. Then about thirty seconds later another train would arrive nearly empty. This morning it happened again. Max got on the nearly empty train and stood up even though seats were available. After several stops, he sat down.

> *It was warm for December. The train was going fast, not slowing down even when going into the turns . . . then it stopped with a thud.*

The sweat started again.

> *A long drawn female HOWL . . . fought its way into his car from the next car. The train wasn't moving. A man moved into Max's car from the adjoining car. He sat down. The man was crying; not sobbing, but tears were rolling down his face . . . A quiet mourning . . . The man stared ahead as the tears rolled.*
>
> *Eventually the man spoke to no one in particular.*
>
> *"A kid fell onto the tracks. The mother won't stop screaming."*

The train was stopped in between stations for ninety minutes, with Max staring at the man's tears and the soundtrack of the mother's howling continuing in a loop.

Eventually a cop entered from the next car.

"We'll be moving shortly, sick passenger. It's nothing."

Max sat down, feeling faint. It had come back. He tried to imagine what the kid was thinking when he hit the tracks, if he smelled the burning steel and electric smoke, if he wondered where his mommy was.

A woman entered his car from the preceding car.

Max's son lived with his ex-wife . . . Six years now.

"Bat-trees! Bat-trees! One dollah!!'

The train kept moving from station to station. Max kept sitting. The illness passed.

He got off at City Hall and went to work. Then he went home, stopping outside his apartment building to smoke a cigarette before going inside. One of the stylists from the shop next door had just finished and was closing up shop. She carried a box. Placing the box on the sidewalk, she unchained her bicycle. Then she picked up the box and mounted the bike. The box balanced unsteadily on the handle bars as she tried to pedal.

"This isn't working," she said to the air as the box fell to the sidewalk.

Max watched as she walked beside the bike, holding the bike with one hand and carrying the box under her left arm. She glided down the street, her legs long and lean clad in black tights. Her long red hair bounced on her shoulders. She kept getting smaller and smaller, then she turned the corner.

He continued to stare down the street even though she was gone.

IN THE MAYOR'S HOUSE
BY PUMA PERL

Ruby fumbled with the clasp of her pearl necklace, a gift from her former mother-in-law. The pearls had outlived both the marriage and her depressed, alcoholic husband; she displayed them only on special occasions.

Damn, you look hot, said the Golden Man as she stepped into the hallway, clad in a black suit and bright red camisole. It was World AIDS Day and she was invited to the Mayor's House, a short walk up East End Avenue. Improbably, the Golden Man, a black trumpet player and bondage enthusiast, resided on East 78th Street and York. It was a source of amusement to them that Ruby, a white social worker, lived in the Avenue D projects.

I love a bitch in a corporate get-up, he continued. *Bend over, just for a second.*

I can't, she replied, slipping into her high-heeled boots, *there's no time.*

Come on, I'll just stick it in you for a minute. Right here, Baby, do it for Daddy.

They stared at each other as she slowly unzipped her pants. He pulled them halfway down, leaving the red garter belt in place, grabbed her ass, and entered her from the rear. She placed her hands against the wall for balance; she knew she wouldn't cum without rubbing her clit against the pillow or her fist, but it felt good just the same . . . maybe she'd duck into the little Mayor's Gracie Mansion bathroom and jerk off.

Fifteen minutes later, Ruby entered the Mayor's House, nodding to the Needle Exchange guy with the Scottish brogue; he'd treated her to lunch once at Buddah, but she hadn't understood a word he'd said, and had left unsure of whether he'd asked for a blow-job or for directions to Bushwick.

He winked at her and headed inside, his long gray-streaked hair beckoning her to follow.

She showed the required pieces of identification and received the requisite red ribbon in return. Nothing much changed from year to year; cheese and crackers, weak Sangria, tepid coffee, and the unfriendly little Mayor, gritting his teeth through endless photo ops, refusing to acknowledge the fact that he was posing with an actual human being by allowing only minimal eye contact and proffering the limpest possible handshake. Every year, she stared him down until he blinked; it was a hollow victory since he exhibited no signs of recognition from one December to the next.

Ruby was asking herself for the thousandth time why she bothered to show up at all when a slight commotion interrupted her thoughts. The photo shoot had begun, and, despite herself, she joined the line, immediately bonding with the most subversive elements she could find. She and a couple of pretty Asian boys amused themselves by jumping up and down, trying to reach the mirrors which were placed above eye level; presumably, the little Mayor's lackeys lifted him up whenever he felt a desire to primp. The light exercise served to loosen her vaginal cavity so that, just as she received the Mayor's flaccid handshake, the Golden Man's cum ran down her leg. She figured the day could not get better than that, so she decided to leave, exchanging mumbles with the Scottish Needle Exchange guy and random hugs with barely remembered colleagues from the front.

What if they knew who I really was? she thought, heading out into a strangely radiant winter day. Prevention specialist, social worker, advocate, curator—and an ex-junkie with an inability to tolerate condoms no matter who she was with—and she'd been with many.

New York City was in remission. After years of *Times* obituaries that printed sentences like "dead from a rotten evil ratfuck disease," a new generation embraced the fantasy of "chronic illness," popped one pill a day, and went on with their lives. Nearly everyone who'd tested in the 80's was either dead or ruined—a few dedicated activists continued to man the barricades, ignored by the slouching hipsters who had claimed the city as their own.

Ruby crossed the street and was immediately surrounded by men in black suits and sunglasses. *Is jaywalking a capital crime?* she managed to ask before passing out.

She awoke sometime later in a bright chintzy room which she recognized as one of the Mayor's guest chambers. Three of the Men in Black guys stood over her. *What the fuck?* she demanded, sitting up, not sure if she was relieved or disappointed to note that she was apparently fully dressed and unmolested.

He wants to seeya, rasped the shortest of the three in a thick Bensonhurst accent. His partners nodded in agreement.

He? As in God himself? asked Ruby, adding, *Gimmee some water or nobody's seeing nobody*. Brooklynese was contagious.

What? Ya think yer in charge over heah? Shorty jutted his chin out menacingly.

Give her some fuckin' water, the middle guy interrupted. *We ain't got all day.* The biggest one remained silent, rocking back and forth like a bouncer. Or a boxer. Ruby was inexplicably attracted to him, even though he'd probably been the one holding the chloroform-soaked rag over her face.

Come on, drink up, we ain't got all day. Naturally, Shorty was the most aggressive of the bunch.

They allowed Ruby to use the facilities to freshen up, although they refused to relinquish her belongings. She finally wheedled a lipstick out of the middle guy; he handed her the wrong shade of red, but she decided not to quibble. She was then led downstairs to an underground office, a section of the Mayor's House not included in public tours and ceremonies.

The Mayor sat stone-faced behind an immense oak desk, surrounded by nervous aides and stone-faced bodyguards, who cut their eyes at her black-suited escorts. The trio, fluent in hulk language, quickly and strategically arranged themselves around Ruby. Weirdly, she felt more protected than threatened by them. *Stockholm Syndrome, already?* she wondered, just as the Mayor opened his mealy mouth.

Siddown, he commanded, in a Bronx accent as thick as Shorty's Brooklynese, a departure from his usual Ivy League, upper-class cadence.

Who's gonna make me? challenged Ruby. Several bodyguards stepped forward in answer to her admittedly stupid question, so she obeyed, perching on the edge of a rose-patterned club chair, staring into the Mayor's eyes. For the first time, without provocation, he stared back.

Ya think I haven't noticed yer behavior the last coupla years? the Mayor asked.

Ruby shrugged.

I been thinkin ya might be just what we need around heah, he continued. His flunkies nodded.

I wouldn't work for you in a thousand years, Ruby replied.

Who said anything about work? Ya won't ever have to work again. I'm talking marriage. They say I need to change my image. You're perfect. As he negotiated, he segued smoothly into his usual speech patterns, bestowing upon her what he imagined was a debonair smile.

Are you fucking nuts? What is this—proposal by chloroform?

It wasn't even real chloroform, Shorty interrupted, *just a little acetone . . .*

Shut the fuck up, hissed Bodyguard Middle, whacking Shorty on the back of the head with a fist the size of a grapefruit.

The Mayor glared at them briefly, and turned back to Ruby, trying to establish a conspiracy of the intelligentsia.

Let's ignore the buffoonery, shall we? he asked. *We have more important matters at hand.*

Yeah, like why you knocked me out with nail polish remover, you midget fuck?

I did no such thing. These fellows were instructed to issue a persuasive invitation to a private conference. Their methods reflect their stupidity and for that, I apologize.

Bodyguard Big remained expressionless, but Ruby could almost smell the steam rising inside of him. He was the hottest psychopath she'd ever seen.

The Mayor placed his square little hands flat against the table. *Time to negotiate!* he announced. *This calls for an intimate tête-à-tête—all of yez, out!* He snapped his manicured fingers and everybody shuffled towards the door, except for Shorty.

But Boss, just in case she tries anything . . . The Mayor cut him off and barked—*Will one of yez get that idiot the hell outta here? She ain't trying nothing. Right?*

Ruby yawned and crossed her legs. She was still a bit groggy and preferred the idea of a strong cup of coffee and a cigarette to wrestling with the Mayor.

Look, said the Mayor, when they were finally alone. *It's a good deal. I get to shock the city into electing me for a fourth term and you can retire and live on easy street. You just show up looking like a rebel and everybody will love me. I'll be Mayor for life! They'll have to change the title to King! We'll be so powerful, we'll secede and run our own country! Wouldn't you like that?*

I think you're an asshole, responded Ruby. *Why would I run a country with you?*

All right, I'm moving too fast. Don't you want to stop working—you can write your poems or whatever it is you people do downtown. You'll be free! Imagine how good it would feel to punch your last time clock!

I can stop working whenever I want to without your help. I'm a Social Worker, remember? We invented entitlements.

But I have the means to set you up for life.

What else you got?

What do you want?

Housing.

Sure! We'll move you right out of those dirty projects . . . I don't know why you live there anyway. What do you want, a condo? Maybe a townhouse?

Not for me! Release all those apartments you've been warehousing! I want two-hundred-thousand units—fifty/fifty low and middle income!

Fifty-thousand—twenty-five/seventy-five!

One-hundred-thousand—forty/sixty!

Done! proclaimed the Mayor, clapping his hands together. *What do you think our wedding song should be?*

Not so fast, Buster, said Ruby. *And we don't need a song. This ain't no romance. I'm never fucking you, I hope you know that.*

Don't flatter yourself, he snarled. *You're not my type. I like those Waspy Blondes, boy you get one of those babies going . . .*

110

You're making me sick, Ruby interjected.

Back to business, agreed the Mayor. *One-hundred-thousand housing units, no song. We got a deal?*

Not yet. Kill those fucking bicycle paths. Let the spoiled brats ride in the street like the rest of us grew up doing.

No problem. I hate hipsters. They never vote, anyway. We finished?

One more thing—trash the Second Avenue subway. They've been building it since 1972! It's never going to happen—use the money for after school programs and senior centers.

All right, all right. But that's it.

What about a cure for AIDS? suggested Ruby.

Come on, said the Mayor, *if I had that, I wouldn't need you. You want the limo to take you home?*

No, I'll grab a cab. Give me some money.

She plucked the fifty he offered out of his hand, and was shown out by the security squad—she palmed her business card to Bodyguard Big and could have sworn she saw a flicker behind the shades.

As soon as she got home, she called the Golden Man.

How'd it go? he asked.

I made a deal to marry the fucking Mayor, she replied.

He got a cure for AIDS?

No, just housing and he's trashing the Second Avenue Subway.

Not bad, not bad.

He's going to kill those ridiculous bike paths, too.

Even better. Now get your fat ass up here by eight. And bring the collar.

Yes, Master.

That's what I like to hear, said the Golden Man, *and don't be late, it stresses out my immune system.*

On my way, Baby, Ruby assured him. *On my way.*

ADVICE FROM SOMEONE USING
BY LISA FERBER

Homer Nebble had already succeeded in being New York City's most lauded obituary writer. This did not change the fact that the landlord of his apartment would never get around to fixing the clanging heater that made Homer's winters a symphonic extravaganza, nor did it inspire him to take his shirt to the tailor when the button got loose, and it certainly did not direct him to pay attention to the ebbs and flows of his mutual funds. And even with the appreciation of millions of the city's inhabitants, the only thing Homer felt would make his life complete was an invitation for soup at Mrs. Glowberg's in apartment 9K.

Homer had started his writing career humbly, composing obituaries out of curiosity and love and offering them to his neighborhood paper, *The West Side Pages*, for free. "Laura Bloomy," he had noted in an early piece, "always replaced the paper in the Xerox machine at her office so the next person would not be stuck. Laura also would discreetly tell a friend if they had buttoned their coat so that it hung unevenly. She will be missed by all who knew her." Writing obituaries had felt like Homer's calling since his adolescence when he had noticed that some people received large writeups and some received tiny ones. Homer felt that everybody's life was worth the same amount and he knew that some day he would be able to put his mark on the world by making it clear that everyone had something to contribute. Homer knew that there was always room to look at someone and say, "Even if they had accomplished nothing else, they were successful because they had accomplished this one thing."

Homer had been raised in a comfortable apartment on 101st Street, just slightly off West End toward Riverside. His parents had sent him to the nearby Columbia University for college so that he could continue living with them and avoid the hedonistic temptations inherent in dorm life.

At Columbia, Homer majored in journalism, which was his way of training to become what the *New York Times* would later call, "This generation's finest obituary writer" and *Crain's New York Business* would name him in their "40 Under 40 List" which was technically reserved for businesspeople but in Homer's case they made an exception because this is how loved he was by his fair city. Homer would gather information about his subjects from interviews with their closest friends, and occasional family members, though he was well aware that family members were not necessarily the persons one might have chosen as trusted companions, so he weighed more heavily on the words of a person's close friends.

Homer had moved back into his parents apartment when he was thirty-five, having moved out at age twenty-five to live with a roommate he'd met through a *Village Voice* ad. The man had told Homer his name was Michael but Homer never quite believed him. Homer had left Michael's home because Michael got way too excited every time

Homer sneezed. Homer had not yet started charging for his obituaries and was earning a little income from working in a neighborhood bookstore run by two brothers, back when the Upper West Side still had a neighborhood bookstore run by two brothers. So he moved in with his folks out of financial desperation, and his parents liked to buy cheese, eat it, and fall asleep on the pullout sofa, while Homer slept on the more comfortable bed.

Homer was growing tired of having no savings and he began to think his talents might be worth something. So he approached Mendrick Desque, editor of *The West Side Pages*, and said, "I hope you don't mind, but I'm thinking about charging."

Since Homer had come on board six years back, readership had gone up 532 percent, and *The West Side Pages* had begun winning Newspaper Association of America awards. Mendrick said, "Homer, we've been hoping you'd finally ask for some payment. You're a grown man and you shouldn't be living with your parents and their whole cheese thing." Mendrick knew about the cheese thing because he had met Homer's parents once when they came to visit him at the office and all they talked about was cheese. Homer wasn't sure if he felt it was bad to live with his parents even though he was a grownup, because it was nice to have people who cared about him and cooked for him and told him to put on a sweater when he was leaving the house. Mendrick continued: "So how about we pay you the rate we pay all our top journalists?" He whispered the rate to Homer even though there was no one around, because Mendrick liked to whisper in order to make a thing feel exciting to him and the listener.

Homer uttered joyfully, "No way!" while gazing into Mendrick's eyes and noticing a tiny eyelash that he resisted mentioning so he wouldn't feel awkward about having gazed so deeply into Mendrick's eyes.

"Yes," Mendrick said firmly. "Way."

The next day, Homer told his parents that he would start looking for a place to live, so that they could have their privacy. It was later on this day that Mildred and Harold Nebble elected to go buy cheese, put it away, lie down, and then die.

When Homer's parents passed away, he wrote their obituary. He wrote it as one piece because Homer had that childlike view of his parents where their whole purpose of being in the world was to be his parents. It wasn't until years later that Homer would realize his parents were just two people who happened to get a kick out each other and then got married and had a kid and it was him.

Homer stayed on in his childhood apartment, after having done a sage cleansing ritual with a woman who claimed to be Wiccan. Homer didn't know if Wiccans were the people who did this kind of stuff but the woman had frizzy gray hair and wore sweatshirts with puffy kitten appliqués and seemed sincere so Homer thought what the hell.

When the lady had finished the cleansing, she had tapped Homer with her magic wand and said, "You, Homer, will some day get to eat the soup you need."

Homer had been craving to eat that soup at Mrs. Glowberg's since he was a child. Mrs. Glowberg was probably in her 80s by now. Her husband had died when Homer was a kid, and her grown children had long since moved out. Homer lived right across the way in 9M and the scent of that soup was like the whole floor was getting a big cozy hug.

Since Homer hadn't told Amy about his yearning, he didn't know if Amy meant her statement literally or metaphorically. The thought of someone reading Homer's mind sort of creeped him out because even though Homer tried to be comfortable with himself, he wasn't sure he really needed anyone knowing every teeny tiny detail.

Also, Homer was not sure if he believed in magic wands, especially Amy's, because he could tell she was using the giant Dunkin' Donuts straw topped with a plush sparkly star that had been on sale at Party Store. He asked, "Do you really think so, Amy? Also, Amy, before you do any more magic stuff with that wand I need to tell you that Amy is not exactly a Wiccan sounding name."

Amy said, "Homer, I didn't mean to tell you I'm Wiccan, that was an error." Amy then realized she had plastered the neighborhood with signs reading, "For a good Wiccan spiritual housecleansing call Amy," so she added, "I mean, I am Wiccan, but not in the sense that you think."

"So what are you, Amy?" Homer asked.

Amy said, "I am your truth. And as I wave this wand, I promise you that you will get to eat the soup you need." At this Amy disappeared into the air, or at least in her mind she did. What really happened was she gazed upward as though receiving a message, then turned and attempted a swift and graceful exit. Unfortunately, she had a little trouble with the door, which stunk for her because she was hoping for a departure that might hold a similar dramatic smoothness to actually disappearing into the air.

Right now Homer had to make a phone call for an obituary about a security guard at a midtown office building. The man's name was Mitch O'Riley and he had worked in the same building as Homer's friend Ben.

Ben's weary voice made it clear he had just woken up. "Hello?"

Homer said, "Ben, hey, glad you're there, it's me." Ben said, "Hey, you're calling about Mitch, right? I wrote something for you but I lost it somewhere in my collection of Bazooka Joe comics." At this point Homer remembered that Ben was a weirdo.

Homer said, "So let's talk about Mitch O'Riley."

"Sure. Mitch O'Riley would make you show your ID even if he'd just seen you leave and go to the magazine store downstairs. So some people disliked him. But I thought he was cool because he was consistent and reliable."

Homer felt a wave of missing his parents and it was hard to know why the pangs would come and go in seemingly arbitrary moments. He said, "Okay, consistent and reliable. Kind of like the sky." Homer felt parents were like the sky. He had known them as part of the world from the moment he got here and he couldn't picture a world without certain things, like the sky, and his parents.

Ben responded, "Maybe like the sky, I guess. So how was your day today, Homer?"

"Well, I saw this woman I kind of know get hit by a car. She had done a spiritual cleansing of my home when my parents died, and she had told me that some day I will get to eat the soup I need."

Then Homer told Ben, "There's something I want on sale at the store."

So Ben hung up. Homer put on his coat and went out in the hall.

In front of the elevator stood Mrs. Glowberg. "Hello, Homer, how are you?"

The elevator opened and the two walked in.

"I'm fine, thank you." Homer knew this would be the moment that she would invite him in. And then Homer would get all that mama-love he knew Mrs. Glowberg's soup contained. "How are you?"

"I'm okay. I just visited the Natts, in 9L. Thirty-two years I've lived here and I've never been inside their home. They are always cooking soup. All the time our floor smells like soup, have you noticed?"

"Um, yeah," Homer said.

Mrs. Glowberg continued, "It's nice, comforting. Me, I'm not such a cook so I like when other people do it. So I've always wanted them to invite me over. But I don't push. So today finally after all this time, they invited me over."

The elevator landed on the first floor, and the door opened. As Homer and Mrs. Glowberg walked out, he asked, "How was the soup?"

She turned and looked at him, and uttered, "Eh."

At this, Mrs. Glowberg turned to approach the mailbox, and Homer slowly walked out of the building, wondering what on earth Wiccan Amy had meant about someday he will get to eat the soup he needs, and then wondering if it was even worth wondering.

HIGH LINE
BY KEVIN DUPZYK

Jerry was sitting in his best clothes, rumpled though they were, looking over his resume one more time. He'd done this before. The door was closed but the last guy had been in there awhile, so he knew that at any second the door would open and it'd be his turn. His palms were sweaty. He needed to get back across the Hudson.

The door opened and the last guy walked out looking like he'd just gotten a colonoscopy. Jerry understood. He was tired of the whole thing: the resume drops, the follow-ups, the follow-ups to the follow-ups, the interviews to no avail, the follow-ups to the interviews to no avail . . . But it had to be done; he'd been out of work for seventeen months now, and dammit, Jerry wasn't going to be out of work for eighteen. He'd go hat-in-hand to every place within reach, if he had to. Suitcase on the subway. Hudson River. Harlem River. He was determined. He was a New Yorker.

The Company Man was standing in the doorway. He took a second to gather himself, looking around as if Jerry wasn't the only person left sitting in the corridor. After an interval, he made sudden, unnerving eye contact. He said, "Well, I guess you're up. Why don't you come on in?"

Jerry got up and went on in.

The Company Man was at least twenty years younger, probably in his early thirties. Maybe even his late twenties. Jerry wasn't sure if the room they sat in was actually his office, but whatever the case, it was antiseptic in its simplicity and décor. He sat down on his side of the desk, but when the man stayed standing, he stood back up. "Mr. . . . uh . . . Frank? Or Mr. Jerry?" the man said, after consulting a roster on his desk. "Which is the last name?"

"Frank," Jerry said. "Frank is the last name: 'Jerry Frank.' Pleased to meet you." He handed over a copy of his resume. "I wasn't sure if you'd have one of these handy, so I brought one for you to look over."

"Thank you," the man said. "Why don't you have a seat?" He motioned towards the seat that Jerry had already sat down in once. Jerry sat down again. Jerry felt a growing wish that this man would die, just drop dead in the middle of the interview.

***

"So then, why don't you tell me a little bit about yourself?" the Company Man said.

"Well, sir, I'm someone who values achievement, and as a result, I look for places where I know that I can contribute." Jerry was well practiced. He continued: "I like being part of a team. I like being on teams that achieve."

"Listen," the young man across from him said, cutting him off as politely as possible, "We do a lot of these interviews. I've done several, even just today. I need you to tell me things about you that are *unique*."

"Okay," Jerry said. He sat quiet and still for just a second. Thinking. This was not how he was used to interviews going. His interview vocabulary had been nullified. And what was there to say about himself? "Okay," he said again. "I, um—Well, let's see. I grew up in the Bronx, but I moved to Hell's Kitchen when I was a kid. Never looked back. My wife Sharon and I, we've got a little garden going for the building we live in and—"

"Mr. Jerry. Sorry. Mr. Frank—"

"Just call me 'Jerry.'"

"Sure. Jerry: How do you expect this to help me choose you for *this* job?"

What did the man want from him? Jerry wondered. What could this younger man understand about him that was unique? He stared stupidly across the table. He knew himself to be a simple man, but he was sure that these answers he'd developed—these means to an end, these skeleton keys of stable income, which Sharon had called his 'Jersey answers'—were *right*.

"Something unique, Jerry, give me something *unique*. And *useful*. Something that will help me *hire* you. Give me something so that I can help you out."

"Like hobbies?" This was all Jerry could think to say.

"Sure, or talents."

"I rather like playing the guitar. I think I'm pretty good at it." He smiled. "That's a hobby *and* a talent."

"Jerry, that's really not—"

"Okay. I'm sorry." He tried again. "I'm very good at taking direction. It makes me a valuable member of any team."

"Jerry, we've already been over this."

"Umm . . . " Jerry looked for something else to say. "Last summer I built a loft bed for my apartment. It really opened things up."

"*This* job, Jerry. Not construction. Not interior design. *How is that relevant?* Tell me something you do that you notice no one else does quite like you."

"Well," Jerry said, "I sort of find myself falling into these existential quandaries."

"Jerry, that's really not—" the Company Man said, starting to reject him again. "Wait. How do you mean?" He squinted across the table. Jerry could feel the man's age pulling on his coattails. This answer had come out of his mouth of its own accord. He had not expected anything but another plea to move on, to give a better answer, but he discerned quite easily that the man's life, his H.R. job as a professional interviewer—it was not conducive to this unexpected turn in the conversation.

Jerry realized that he did in fact want the man to die, but of extreme youth, like a chick fallen from the nest or a calf separated from its herd on the high plains.

"You want an example?"

"Sure, give me an example."

"Well, I was walking through High Line Park a few days ago," Jerry started. Then he paused. "You know High Line Park?"

"Eh . . . no, I don't," the man said.

"It's this elevated park just South of my neighborhood. It's—"

"Elevated?" the Company Man asked. "Right," he said, apparently to himself.

"Yes, elevated," Jerry said. "It used to be an El track."

"'El?' 'El,' as in . . . ?"

"Well, '*El*evated.'" Jerry said. He wasn't sure if this was reflecting well or poorly on him. "'El' as in 'elevated train.' You see, back in the 30's, they built a train for deliveries to the West Side. They built it right above the city blocks so that it wouldn't interfere with anything on the street level. All the buildings received their deliveries on the second floor—or at least, that's how I imagine it worked." Jerry smiled at the thought. "It's really kind of an amazing and beautiful thing, when you think about it. Novel."

"Right," the Company Man said again, nonplussed. *"Existential."* He rolled the word around on his tongue. Jerry kept his mouth shut for a moment, but he was encouraged to continue: "Go on," his interviewer said, "I still want to hear about these *'existential* quandaries.'"

Jerry stayed quiet for another beat. He wasn't sure how to proceed. "So it's this nice park, it runs for several blocks, and because it's on an elevated platform, it has all these great views of the Hudson. There's lots of couples that walk up there. There's benches and chairs all over the place, you can sit with your lady and watch the sunset. It's very romantic." He paused to think to himself. "It's like—you know that old Times Square picture of the sailor and the nurse from the end of World War II? It's like that. Like maybe this is the *new* New York." As Jerry said this, he realized that he didn't hate New Jersey so much as he very completely loved New York City. It was always changing, always adapting, always staying beautiful and relevant. It was resilient. Train tracks become a park. Towers go down and then back up. It was why he knew he could continue this job search until it was finally fruitful.

"And that's it? That was your quandary?" the Company Man asked.

"No, of course not. That's not a quandary. That's like a—a *supposition.*"

The Company Man sighed. "Alright, Jerry, I'll be honest with you: I don't know what an 'existential quandary' *is.*"

"Well," Jerry said, taking great pleasure, thinking that perhaps he was gaining some ground on his interviewer, "That's basically the fundamental difference between New Yorkers and you kids on this side of the river."

"What?"

"Never mind." A beat. "It's just hard to—an 'existential quandary' is sort of strange. I guess . . . I guess it's this feeling you get when you're not sure if who or what you are *matters*. Like maybe it's out of your control, and if it is, then—well, then what's it all about? You know what I mean?"

"I think I do, actually," the Company Man said, with great sincerity, and with this new turn the older man realized—with a very human bit of discomfort—that he *wasn't* gaining the upper hand in the interview, because this had ceased to be *about* the interview, but rather that the change he felt in the room was a strange sort of intimacy growing between him and the younger man on the other side of the desk.

"So here was my existential quandary: I was walking along High Line Park, surrounded by all these couples. I was thinking about Sharon, and the streets we walked when we were just kids. We'd walk up Wall Street and wonder if we'd ever know wealth; we'd walk the Bronx, where I grew up, and we'd walk the streets of Red Hook, where she grew up, and we'd wonder if we'd ever know poverty again. We were like these couples on the High Line, but in our own time. And I was leaning against the railing—not looking at the Hudson, but East, back across the city—and thinking about that: the New York of Sharon and me, and the New York of now. I was standing there quietly when I became aware of some nearby commotion, and looking over I saw that there was a photographer taking a picture of a young couple. And I realized that I was in the background of this picture."

"What was this, like, engagement photos or something?"

"I think so, yes," Jerry said.

"And that bothered you, to be in the picture?" the Company Man asked. "That made you feel—how'd you say it?—like you weren't sure if you *matter*?"

"I guess I just started to think about the fact that I'd be in the picture for*ever*. Not with Sharon, and not in my neighborhood, or on the streets of the borough where I grew up—just me, alone, in a two-year-old park, an afterthought in someone else's photo. And I'll be there, always."

"I guess that is sort of strange," the Company Man said. He held his body in an unnatural posture.

"I kind of imagine myself in some photo album in two hundred years, yellowing and curling into something grotesque."

"I've felt like that before, I think. It was in college. I played a little ball, and there was a big game where I made a fielding error and it was listed in the box score. And I had this thought: 'That error is going to be next to my name every time someone tries to find out what happened in that game.'"

"Exactly," Jerry said.

"It's like there's some eternal ledger and in it next to my name that's what there is: 'Error, seventh inning.'"

The two men sat and thought of all of their eternities.

"You won't yellow and curl, you know," the Company Man said, breaking the silence.

"What?"

"Well, I mean—" the man said, "I mean, it was digital, right? So you'll be in that camera in ones and zeroes . . . "

"Is that supposed to make me feel better?" Jerry asked. "Am I supposed to take comfort in that?"

"Well, it's almost like you'll live forever. Pristine and intact."

"I hate to tell you this, kid, but nothing lives forever. Not you, not me. Not even New York. Not even The City."

"It'll have its own chapter in that Book though, and you'll be there with it," the young man said, and surely what followed was a statement of his youth: "Maybe you just belong there."

"Maybe," Jerry said.

"Just think: If it's out of your control, and who and what you are don't matter—there's far worse places to be than New York City."

Jerry expelled air slowly through the corner of tight lips.

***

On his way out, he thanked the receptionist and took a mint from the glass bowl on her counter. She was young and pretty and very nice to him. After he unwrapped the mint and popped it into his mouth, she even offered to take the wrapper and throw it away for him. He declined. He thought she probably felt sorry for him.

Jerry took the elevator down a floor, dropped off his visitor's pass at the security desk, and walked outside into the sunlight, across the small plaza, and over to the river's edge. There was The City, just across it, and tucked in amongst the buildings, long and lean, was High Line Park.

Jerry turned slowly turned around, tracing the line of the Hudson down from the North, tracing the running edge of Jersey City and its own tall towers. He thought: Another eponymous city, and so different from ours. He thought: I will not be getting this job.

Soon he was facing the shiny glass façade of the building he'd interviewed in, and a floor up, through open blinds, he realized he could see the young Company Man. The man gathered his things and slipped them into his bag, and then he paused and looked out the window. He was looking in Jerry's exact direction, but his eyes were opaque. He was fixed in the window, framed perfectly, and he loosened his tie and unbuttoned his top button. The look on his face was one of incredible weariness.

Jerry imagined the man's despair. He had felt it. It was hard not to. In fact, he thought, everyone felt it at some point, and for their own reasons; perhaps these reasons were the very things that defined them. And for Jerry, it was The City that did this to him. There was the low of being left without a purpose and the high of knowing that such things existed; purposes that walked through Central Park and across the Brooklyn Bridge and through the gates of Yankee Stadium and, yes, even along the old tracks of High Line Park. These were all a part of The City. Maybe, Jerry thought, that's what he would be in the photograph: a specter of another New York, just a shadow in the wake of the young couple's love, but not without consequence.

With this thought he let his eyes glaze and, like someone turned his focus ring, the Company Man's weary and hopelessly intact face faded from view, and instead, reflected on the window of the interview room, Jerry saw the skyline of The City.

NOVALIS
BY JANET HAMILL

> *The Night is here —*
> *My soul's enraptured —*
> *The earthly day's past*
> *And you're mine again.*
>
> —Georg Friedrich von Hardenberg

It was a rainy day in late September. The wind was nasty, getting down around the neck, up the sleeves, and under the waist of my new leather jacket. In the open space of Times Square, the light offered little contrast to the dimness of the subway stairwell from which I emerged. It was my birthday, and I'd elected to cut classes at Roslyn High School and spend the money my father mailed me at Lou Tannen's Magic Shop.

I flipped up my collar and walked up Broadway, catching a glimpse of John Wayne blowing smoke rings out of the big cigarette billboard overhead. In the steady grey drizzle, a few guys my age huddled together looking at Cuban boots in Florsheim's window. At the Howard Johnson's a group of housewives from Jersey, jostled their way through the door, no doubt intent on having a grilled cheese or BLT before seeing Burton and Taylor in *Cleopatra*.

The Birds was playing at the movie house next door to Lou Tannen's. In the display stills outside the theatre, Tippi Hedren and Rod Taylor locked eyes over a caged bird, hundreds of sparrows flew through a fireplace, and crows swooped and attacked a group of school children. Definitely, *The Birds* was the film I most wanted to see of the new releases. But that would be another day.

The warm air in the vestibule at 1540 Broadway was a welcome change from the wet street. I took the stairs to the second floor and opened the door with the panel of frosted glass stenciled with a gold top hat and cane. Inside, there was one customer for whom the one salesman, Jack Miller, was demonstrating the *Zombie Ball*. I'd run into Jack over the Labor Day Weekend on the boardwalk in Coney Island. We were both there to catch Novalis's act. During an intermission, he came up to me and told me I might want to stop by the shop and see the new items that had come in.

Jack gave a wink to indicate that he'd be with me momentarily. I signaled not to hurry. Ordinarily, when I visited Tannen's it was on a Saturday afternoon and the place was mobbed. I'd never seen it on a Monday morning, quiet and near empty, and for the first time I was getting a good look at the mural and the posters on the walls. Houdini in chains. Blackstone and Thurston in formal evening dress and black capes. Chung Ling Soo defying bullets. Framed handbills for *The Hour of Darkness* at the Egyptian Hall Bazaar, the *Wonders of the Enchanted Palace*, and *Davenport's Spirit Cabinet*. The mural was total kitsch but wonderful. In lurid red, yellow, orange and pink paint mellowed with age, it depicted a winged genie hovering over a snake charmer and a silver urn emanating wisps of smoke. It was the perfect backdrop for a place that was part funhouse, part treasure trove.

The customer was having difficulty grasping the mechanics of the *Zombie Ball*. He repeatedly asked Jack to perform the trick, and each time Jack cheerfully obliged. He showed both sides of the foulard outstretched between his hands over a polished metal ball resting on a stand. He covered the ball with the foulard for a second. Then the ball rose through the air and disappeared behind his shoulder. It was one of my favorite tricks to perform at kid's parties, though I doubted my performances had Jack's panache.

While the demonstration continued, I checked out the display case labeled *Club and Stage Magic—New Arrivals*. Side by side, with printed cards describing their effects, were such items as *Great Brahman Rice Bowls*, *Rosini's Robot Wand*, *Flames of Aladdin* and *Snows of Kimalatong*. For their names alone, I wanted to buy each one and keep them in mint condition in their original boxes in my bedroom where I could marvel at them whenever I wanted.

The guy for whom Jack was demonstrating finally got it. He left the shop, having laid out nineteen-fifty for a deluxe model, seven-inch *Zombie* and an additional two-fifty for a red foulard to go with it. With a satisfied look on his face, Jack closed the cash register and came over to where I was standing.

"See anything you like, Joe?"

"Well," I said, "I like everything, but I can't afford it all."

He asked me how much I wanted to spend. My father had sent me a twenty, but I didn't want to blow it all at Tannen's.

"Fifteen," I said.

"Fifteen. No problem." He slid open the back of the display case. "*Great Brahman Rice Bowls*, *Sands of the Desert*, and

The Famous Egg Bag are all less than fifteen. *Nesto Candles*—for one hand only—is ten."

"How much is the *Wrist Guillotine?*"

"Seventeen-fifty."

"And the *Fire Bowl?*"

"Twenty-one."

"Okay," I said, "let me see the rice bowls and *Flames of Aladdin.*"

Jesus! Decisions. Both items were twelve-fifty, and whereas the *Great Brahman Rice Bowls* was a new version of a venerable stage trick, the gaudy brass Aladdin's lamp was irresistible. I read the trick's description on the ornate printed card: *Really sensational! A dream come true! As though a real GENIE were present, the flames leave the lamp and FLOAT in mid-air!!!* I *had* to have it. With the money left over, I bought a new lucite wand to replace the one some brat had walked off with at a Glen Cove birthday party.

Jack Miller took my money and put the wand and the *Flames of Aladdin* in a shiny black bag with Tannen's cool, gold printed logo. He handed me my change, and taking me by surprise, asked if I wanted to join him for lunch. It threw me off a little. I mean I hardly knew the guy. Some of the other dudes who frequented the shop told me they thought Jack might be gay. I came from a white bread Long Island town where anyone who was queer never copped to it. So what would I say if he came on to me? I thought a minute and then my mind cleared. What the fuck? It didn't matter. Jack was a good guy who was full of the fun and mystery of magic tricks. Fact is, I didn't think there was anything wrong with being gay. The only people who said so always turned out to be assholes. Fuck 'em.

Jack called me out of my silent but decisive meditation. "Hey Joe! Lunch?"

"Sure Jack, lunch would be cool."

"Great! You pick the place."

Other than Howard Johnson's, I was only familiar with one other place in the neighborhood—the place where my father and I ate before going to boxing matches or hockey games at the Garden. "How about the Alamo Chili Café?"

"The Alamo it is! Just let me close up and we're off to eat Mexican."

Down on the street, there were a few more people hastening in the rain on their lunch breaks. Jack Miller opened a big green umbrella and welcomed me to share it with him. Jack was almost a foot shorter than I was. I bent to get under, then we were off.

"Yah know Joe," Jack said, half trotting to keep up with my pace, "We can make this a leisurely lunch. On a Monday afternoon with weather like this, the shop's dead. Lou's down in Miami. So we can relax and shoot the breeze."

At Forty-seventh Street we crossed Broadway, heading east. The Alamo Chili Café was between Sixth and Seventh, in the middle of the block. It had been awhile since I'd been there, but *nothing* had changed. The framed page from the *New York Mirror* was there near the entrance, with Dan Parker's article about Casey Stengel eating at the Alamo. The long, black wood bar was still on the left, and the red malt shop-style booths on the right. It was a simple place with a funky, B-movie Mexican look.

Only one or two people sat at the bar and all the booths were empty. I led the way to the one in the rear beneath a yellow velvet sombrero with filigree trimming. We slid into opposite seats, and a guy came over to take our orders. He spoke slowly and had a sleepy Tijuana look in his eyes. I ordered my favorite—spaghetti with chili and two tamales. Jack ordered the same and asked if he could have a drink while we waited for our meal.

"Si, señor," said the Mexican, with a definite Rio Grande accent. "What will it be?"

"Scotch on the rocks?"

"Scotch on the rocks, si. He turned his glance to me. And you, señor?"

"I'll have a coke."

The waiter walked away and both Jack and I were silent, settling in after our rain rush. The beverages arrived quickly, and once Jack had a sip or two of his scotch, he started talking in his Noo Yawk voice. I was all ears for what he had to say.

"So, you're a Novalis fan. Probably, I should put that in the past tense. You know he's gone missing. Since Labor Day, no one's seen him anywhere."

"No kiddin'?" I said. "Man, that's weird."

Jack shifted into a more serious tone. "It is. He really has disappeared into thin air. Gone without a trace. And this morning two police detectives came into the shop to quiz me. Thank god Bernie's in Miami! I didn't know what he would want me to tell them. I doubt that I know much more about what happened than the cops. From talking to the detectives, I got the bad impression that they're working on a murder case. I had my suspicions, too. But I wasn't thinking it was that bad."

His words stung me, shocked me. I'd only discovered Novalis at the beginning of the summer. A friend of mine had taken me to see him perform in a dive on Surf Avenue. He was truly amazing. A master illusionist with a cool, almost indifferent stage manner and leading man looks. He looked like a young Robert Mitchum, only shorter, slighter, and even shaggier. I wondered what the hell he was doing in a dive in Coney Island. He was so fucking good. Good enough for the *Ed Sullivan Show*. Good enough for Broadway with tickets sold out six months in advance. Later in the summer he moved into the Squire Room, a slightly less shabby club. It was a step up, but still. . . .

"Who would want to kill Novalis?" I felt very strange asking Jack that question.

"Christ, I don't know. He was involved in all kinds of freaky entanglements. We were supposed to get together that night, after his last show of the summer. I waited for him in his dingy room in the Sea Beach Hotel. The last show was scheduled to end at eleven-thirty. I smoked half a pack of Luckies waiting for him. When he still hadn't shown at one o'clock, I took the subway back to Manhattan.

"In the morning, Anita, the daughter of the guy who runs the Squire, called me at home to ask if Novalis was with me. Much to Daddy's distaste, Anita had become Novalis's stage assistant and lover during the Squire Room engagement. She was crazy about him.

"Anita said there'd been a bizarre twist in the *Substitution Trunk* trick at the end of the last show. You've seen the act. The assistant gets in a box, which is chained up and secured with a real steel lock. The box is lowered into a huge travel trunk, which is also chained and locked. Novalis raises a curtain around himself and the trunk. With a count of *one, two, three* the curtain drops, and, *voila*, there stands the assistant, free and out of the trunk. The magician is gone. The trunk is still locked and tied. The assistant opens the trunk and then the box. Out steps Novalis, having switched places with the assistant in an instant. Right? That's the trick. A real pisser. But when Anita opened the box there was no one inside to step out!"

"Thanks," I said, as the waiter placed a large plate of spaghetti with chili and tamales in front of me. Jack looked at his serving with something less than relish and ordered another scotch.

"Anita was completely freaked. Novalis had never said anything about vanishing. She had to think fast and improvise her way off the stage. No one knows how he could possibly have exited the trunk because his methods were all his own. No one else was in on the secret—sure as hell not me. Afterwards, no one saw him back stage or in the dressing room. Anita and the guys who work for her old man made a frantic round of Novalis's regular Coney haunts. He wasn't with Fat Tina. He wasn't with Phil, who operates the Cyclone. He wasn't at the tattoo parlor or any of the bars. By the time they got to the Sea Beach, I was long gone. Back home asleep."

Jack Miller's second drink arrived and he took a lusty gulp. "It was bizarre. But then again, it wasn't a complete surprise. I'd come to anticipate the unexpected with Novalis. My first thought was that his disappearance was his idea of a great joke, the mysterious grand finale of the season. But after a week passed and still no one had seen or heard from him, I began to get anxious. I began to think about him committing suicide."

I must have been looking clueless because Jack repeated himself.

"That's right, Joe. I began to think suicide, because it made sense. Knowing Novalis as well as I did, it made sense. You see, he confided in me. He told me things he would never tell anyone else. I knew he wanted out of his relationship with Anita and out of his business association with her mobbed-up family. He felt obliged to them because of the cash they'd put into his act. Big money for top draw stuff like the *Substitution Trunk* and the *White Cargo Cage*. For once, he had a first class act and he was starting to attract serious attention. You could smell success and big recognition coming his way. But, yah know, I think the idea of sudden fame scared him, that and the fact that he would owe it to Anita and her father.

"No, fame and wealth didn't fit into Novalis's overall picture of things. It would have been too much of an infringement on his freedom. It would have cramped his style. You gotta understand, Joe, he was a drifter at heart, and I think he wanted to keep it that way. Drifting from place to place, with nothing but an old obsession to keep him company."

I was amazed that Jack was telling me all this. Like I said, I hardly knew the guy, and we were getting into pretty deep waters.

"Do you know what Novalis's real name is? Homer Sinclair Nash. You believe it? It's a southern thing. I think his family has money. He's from somewhere in Georgia. He took the name Novalis after a poet he was hung up on. Once he told me that he thought he might be the reincarnation of this poet. The real Novalis was an eighteenth-century German. He died at the age of twenty-nine, just a few years after the death of the woman he loved. Do you know how old our Novalis is? Twenty-nine! And he'd been engaged to a girl who died tragically about eight years ago."

I leaned forward, an enthralled kid listening to Jack Miller talk about life and death.

"It happened down south. Homer was just starting out. He wasn't 'Novalis' then; he was just 'Homer, Master of Mystery.' He'd hooked up with a carnival in a little coast town near Savannah. One summer night a beautiful girl from the local high school came to his show with some of her girlfriends. Her name was Donna. She was the daughter of the local sheriff. Homer was usually indifferent to his admirers, but he noticed this girl. From the stage, he looked over at her throughout his act. Each time their eyes met. After the show, Donna separated herself from her friends and waited for him. As Novalis describes it, it was a once in a lifetime experience. Standing before her and looking into her eyes, he said, was like being in the presence of the other half of his soul.

"Shortly after their first meeting, Donna and Homer became lovers. It was the first time for Donna, and it wasn't easy for her. She had to steal away from her friends and family and lie about where she was going. She was terrified that her father would find out about Homer and their secret trysts. By the end of the summer she was pregnant. Novalis wanted to marry her. They planned to elope when the carnival packed it up. Then something awful happened.

"For all his love of his soulmate, Novalis couldn't control his sexual appetites. Women and men were drawn to him like moths to a flame, and he couldn't reject their offerings. One night Donna came earlier than usual for a rendezvous. She went behind Novalis's tent and found him balling one of the carnie chicks. She let out a scream and ran out into the crowd on the fairgrounds. Novalis took off after her. When he caught up with her, she was standing in a seat stopped at the top of the Ferris wheel. He pleaded with her to calm down, to sit down, to come down and talk to him. He shouted that everything was all right, nothing had changed. She must have been devastated, in a state of shock, because she began to rock the seat, violently, back and forth. Whether by accident or intent she tumbled out and fell to her death. After that night, Homer Sinclair Nash fled the town and the carnival and started a new life as Novalis. He had the names Novalis and Donna tattooed in a black heart on his chest. Then he started drifting up the coast."

Jack waved to the waiter and raised his glass. He hadn't touched his spaghetti, chili or tamales. I'd finished my plate and was still hungry. I ordered the one item on the menu offered as "dessert"—guava jelly and cream cheese on saltine crackers.

Jack went on with a faraway look on his face. "I first met Novalis about a year ago when he started coming into the shop. He wanted books on the great illusionists and the history of stage magic. Right away, I sensed something very special about him. We became friendly. We started having lunch together, just like you and I are now. Novalis needed a confidant. I don't think he'd ever had someone to speak to about what really mattered to him. For whatever reason, he decided that I was the one to listen to his story.

"I remember one night in particular. He was still working Surf Avenue. We took a walk on the boardwalk. He was going on and on about infinity and the place where the night sky and the ocean come together. He said he wanted to go there and be reunited with Donna. He was writing a lot of poetry then. We stopped beneath a lamplight and he took a poem out of his pocket to read to me. You know, Joe, a guy like me doesn't know much about poetry, but I thought it sounded pretty good. Different. Distinctive. It was all about love, sacrifice, the night. He was very much into 'the night.' In retrospect, I think the poetry I heard that night foretold everything that's come down."

Jack Miller reached into his pocket and took out something handwritten on a sheet of yellow legal paper.

"I think this is Novalis's suicide note. It was in his room the night he disappeared. I think he asked me to meet him there, fully knowing he'd never come, but knowing I'd find this poem. If you don't mind, I'd like you to read it."

I felt privileged and nervous at the same time. Goose bumps rippled all over me. I put down my cracker and picked up the paper. In small, blue, block letters, printed with a ballpoint pen, I read . . .

HYMN TO THE NIGHT

Down at last to the sea
At last to drown my soul

The distant lights of the carnival
The noise of the crowd
The notes of the calliope
Rise high above the waves

On a pedestal shell
My Venus comes
With open arms
To sleep, her long sleep

With loving eyes
Forgiveness
I shed my shirt —
the veined wings of a mourning dove —

And offer myself to the Night

It wasn't Corso but it sounded okay to me. It sounded pretty sad, like it might have been a farewell. "Yeah, I see what you mean," I said. "I can see why you would think these were his last words."

Jack Miller was visibly pleased, maybe moved by my reaction. "You know," he said, "once I'd come to that conclusion, about a week after the disappearance I went out to Coney Island. The weather was like it is today and the beach was deserted. I had to walk way out past the last pier before I found what I was looking for—Novalis's translucent, dark blue shirt, embroidered with white stars. It was washed up under the boardwalk."

"You're fuckin kiddin' me! Did you tell the cops? Do they know about the poem? Or Anita? Does she know anything about the shirt or the poem?"

"No. Exposing the secret of Homer Sinclair Nash's final deception doesn't seem right to me. I don't know if you get this, but to expose it would be unpardonable. Everything I've told you belongs to Novalis and Donna wherever they are."

I saw his point—but hadn't he just exposed the secret to me?

Our lunch had now taken up the better part of two hours and I was feeling edgy because I had a train to catch at the Long Island Railroad Station. Jack Miller finished his drink and signaled the waiter to bring the check. "This is on me, Joe," he said. He thanked me for listening to his story and urged me to visit the shop sometime again, real soon.

It was still raining like hell when we parted outside the Alamo and the sky was getting dark. To keep my new treasures from getting wet, I put the shiny black bag with the *Flames of Aladdin* and the lucite wand under my jacket. I turned up my leather collar and walked as quickly as I could to the nearest subway. I couldn't wait to be seated on the train, heading back to Roslyn, trying to understand all that had been told to me. I felt like I was ten years older, maybe more.

SEE/SAW SOMETHING
BY PETER CARLAFTES

Staring up the tunnel for the faintest hint of light I can see the disconnection from what used to be my life. Love and all pursuit is a future of blank. Now the train shows itself—so there's direction for a moment.

I should've been at work but I covered my shift because I felt like hanging with Lateef on his truck. It's an old book-mobile he's pimped out to look like a giant street cart and parks outside clubs in the meatpacking district and creates wild snacks to sell drunks.

I board the downtown 6 and take the first seat on my right. The car's empty at 8 o'clock on Friday night—Hold on! I pull myself up to make sure it's not some ghost train and, satisfied by the sight of other riders fore and aft, I sit back and embrace solitude.

Lateef concocts these crazy things, like—hot dogs shaped like soft, salted pretzels, and pretzels that look like hot dogs and a bun. I've helped him twice before and we really hit it off. We met about a month ago outside Zuccotti Park.

Here's comes 86th Street. And probably eight little men playing panpipes.

The train stops. The doors open. No one gets on. OK. The doors close. I'm used to such rejection. No. That isn't really true. I'm used to being alone.

Hell. In most circles, I'd be considered nuts to take off work to have a few laughs instead. Well. These days—laughs come too far between. And while it may seem to some that my ducks were out of order, the crucial factor which enabled me to make such a foolish choice—was I haven't paid rent for over 27 months.

Along comes 77th Street comprised of flickering faces, yet once the doors slide open not a one steps in the car. Here I am all by my lonesome. Just like in my building.

See. Four years ago, my landlord had this greedy little notion he could chase out every tenant and then triple all his rents. Well. Four years later, I remain the last man standing. But after daily loud construction through my walls from all directions, I'm glad there's no place like home. The only good thing that's happened to me lately's been finding her again. Josie. Maybe it was meant to be. No way of knowing—yet.

She was on the top floor—5. I'm still on 2, as then. You know. We'd run into each other in the hall and started talking. On one of those occasions, she came into my room. It went like this awhile, but she moved and we lost track after that—until last Monday afternoon, when her long red hair caught my eye on Lex pushing a baby carriage.

Thin face. Green eyes. Sexy. Slightly taller. We put four years behind us in a minute and a half. Then Josie introduced me to her six-month-old, Coquette. Another redhead. What a cutie. She asked if I could babysit tomorrow (Tuesday morning). She had to deal with "issues" concerning Coquette's father, whose status she left at—Out of

Our Lives. They lived just off Park on 104th. I told Josie, "Why Not."

68th Street/Hunter College. Reminds me of when, as a young man, I used to sit in on a lot of classes, but none held my interest long enough to really want to become someone else.

I lean out the door and watch people get on, only not on the car that I'm in! The doors slide shut. Something must be wrong. Then dropping to my seat, I caught first sight of the bag. By the far doors, catty-cornered to my right.

OK. I'm on some inane new TV show. Where all of them pop up from inside the seats the second I touch the bag. I mean—it's been here all this time. There's no way in frozen hell I could've missed it.

A classy, light-brown men's calfskin tote. I'd say 14 x 20, with finely-stitched straps. I think I've seen one in the Hermes store before. You see. With constant noise surrounding my apartment, I wind up spending lots of time mind-shopping on Madison Avenue; you know—like not really buying. And I work on the Avenue, too—so I'm a guy who knows fine leather. That bag costs 1500 bucks.

The train stops at 59th. I stand up once again, keeping one eye on the bag. The cars in front and behind are at least half full. And Nobody Gets On Mine. It's time to ask myself the question that I ask in these types of situations: What Would Bobby Short Do?

You see, I worked with Bobby Short for 13 years and a sweeter, nicer man you'll never meet. So—Whose judgment better to draw upon for moral support than his? Now the doors close, but the train's being held, so I've time to sort out my dilemma.

I'm a waiter at The Carlyle and the prestige of that itself has lent a certain peace of mind to other aspects of my life.

Even after the landlord started tearing down the building with me in it—still, I held my ground. But ever since June, when the water went off, I couldn't sleep very well—which left me fearing the unknown.

Then I met this girl who worked at Barney's in cosmetics sometime in mid-July. Her name was Cleo. Well. She came to see me once for lunch and soon we started going to her place and all I really felt was great relief. Insomuch—that, after the thrill between Cleo and I came and went, I made this deal with her and her roommate to sleep on their couch twice a week for a hundred bucks, which worked out especially well for me until they changed the lock without a word in late September. And who could blame them? That's when I started thinking about Zuccotti Park.

Now—as the train goes so do I and sit directly across from the bag under one of those "If You See Something, Say Something" signs. I'm pretty sure at this point that Bobby Short would bail and catch the express, but I'm extremely stubborn; plus I like the bag. Plus I've never come to terms with that mentality. Telling doesn't cut it in the City. You open the bag. Maybe you find something good. And maybe the next day, they find you floating in the river. Doesn't matter either way. You have to take your shot. That's what drew me to Occupy Wall Street. These people were taking their shot.

I bought a cheap tent from a sporting goods shop and went down there in October and found a place to put it up. Then spent a few nights sleeping next to others under tarps. Some of them complained about having things stolen; which got me thinking—if they couldn't figure out a way to stop small scale theft, how could they ever end the reign of corporate greed? I gave the tent to three Norwegians and spent November it a hostel. Lucky me. The cops moved everybody out the same month. The best thing was hooking up with Lateef and his truck.

The train pulls into 51st Street. No one else gets on the car. I'm standing by the bag as the doors close. Staring at the Say Something sign.

Worse case scenario: I open the bag—the bag blows up; I sing old tunes forever with Bobby Short and Cole Porter. It's a win/win proposition.

Best case scenario: I sell the bag on Craigslist and buy Josie and Coquette something nice. Hell. Christmas is only three weeks away. Maybe buy them a tree. I'm sure the kid could use some diapers. Hold on. As much as I'd like to pick up again with Josie, there's no need to get this far ahead of myself. I'm too worn out from the last six months.

Next case scenario: Instead of catching the L over to 8th from Union Square, I get off at Grand Central and check out what's in the bag—then I'll meet up with Lateef a little later. Simple. I pick up the bag and it's a Ferragamo. Damn! I could've sworn it was Hermes. Well. Here comes the moment critique.

I cross directly to the nearest bench and set the bag down on a seat. Then delicately undo the snap. Pausing, I sweep a quick glance around and, using both hands, open the bag—which suddenly lights up exposing this odd mechanism with a barrel pointing out. Then a sharp voice from within commands, "Don't Move Or You'll Be Tased!"

There's quite a spell of silence. I ask the bag, "What Should I Do?"

"Be Quiet," said the voice from the bag—adding, "Nod If You Understand."

What else could I do? I nod.

The voice tells me, "Just Follow My Instructions."

After another long spell, I ask the bag, "What Instructions?"

The voice sighs, "I Thought You Understood."

"Huh? Oh Yeah—Right." I nod again.

The voice says, "Good. Pick Up The Bag. Then Walk To The Downtown End Of The Platform. After The Last Set Of Stairs Turn Right. You Will Be Facing An Elevator. Stand By The Door. Then Wave At The Man To Your Left Behind The Glass In The Dispatchers Booth. The Door Will Open. Get On. And Just Remember—The Taser Mechanism WILL Trigger If You Try To Drop The Bag. Understood?"

I nod. The voice says, "MOVE!"

I lift the bag and start walking. Well. They say you'll see it all if you live in this city long enough. I wonder if I'll make The Police Blotter.

Here's the stairs. Turn right. There's the elevator. Look left. There's the guy behind the glass. He looks like Jerry Orbach on boredom pills. I wave at him. He nods. The door opens. The guy points. The car seems like it's on last legs.

The voice says, "Down We Go!"

I read once over 20 floors exist in this place below street level. With miles of abandoned tracks. And even colonies of people. I can't be sure. I've never seen them. We're right at floor 10. Strange. Not worried in the least. One thing I do know: Been looking for a change. 11th floor. Might be a blessing.

Now the elevator stops at an unmarked floor between 12 and 14 with a jolt and opens on a stale, dank square of cement painted white. There's an old steel grey desk straight ahead, with a thin black man wearing blue and grim look behind a screen lit more brightly than the fixture above.

I ask, "Is this really the 13th Floor?"

He snaps, "There ain't no such thing! Come On!"

Meaning me. Meaning now.

I go in. The rickety door clangs shut.

The man points to his right, "Put the bag on the floor by the desk."

Which I do. Then ask, "Are you the voice from the bag?"

He almost breaks. But snaps, "My name's Officer Calvin Morris. You sit down and zip it up!"

There's a dark brown folding chair by the metal door farther right, which I take and watch Morris click a mouse. Seems like a nice enough guy. Mid-thirties; Dreamer.

Not too many coming true.

I ask him, "You want my ID?"

"Nah," Morris shrugs. "We use Facial Recognition." Then leans back smugly and reads from the screen. "Name: Benjamin Cartafte. Born: 1967. 5'10". Hair: Brown. Eyes: Blue." Then he shoots a quick look to make sure that they're blue and, when rest assured, he continues, "Address: 170 E. 100th Street. Damn! You work at The Carlyle?

When I nod, Morris frowns, "Then what was your ass doing down in Zuccotti Park?"

Right then, the metal door swings open and a short, Asian man wearing black round-rimmed glasses and light brown fatigues quickly crosses behind Morris and asks, "What's his story?"

I challenge, "Why not just ask me?"

"Because we know in our position that a perp will always lie," responds the short man, then looks at me more closely and lights up, "Weren't you in my Forensics class at John Jay right after 9/11?"

Startled, I say, "Yeah—I guess. But I was only sitting in."

He smiles, shaking his head, "Wow. You look exactly the same." Then asks Morris, "What's his name?"

Morris tells him, "Ben", and then to me, "He's Sergeant

Cheung. Ben here works at The Carlyle, Sarge. Probably makes more bread than us both put together. Yet the Dude's been hanging out down in Zuccotti Park."

I interject, "I only slept there a few nights. I've been having grief with my apartment."

"What grief?" asks the Sergeant.

I tell him, "You don't want to know."

"That's where you're wrong," the Sergeant plies. "We're here to help."

"Yeah. We're your Friends," chimes in Morris.

Hmm. GoodCop/Good Cop's working. I spill my tale of woe. About no water (thus no toilet) since last summer, and the last two years of banging starting 6 o'clock each morning and the stairs blocked with the clutter and no heat so far this winter, and the story of my landlord doing anything he wants.

"OK—Up!" the Sarge tells Morris, "Let me see what I can do."

Morris stands. The Sergeant takes his seat and types. Morris quips, "You think I'm bad? This dude's a monster!"

The Sergeant reads off the screen, "170 E. 100th Street. Owner: C. Scaringella."

"We call him Mighty Joe Cheung," boasts Morris.

The Sergeant keeps reading, " First and Second Court Hearing Postponed. Third court hearing: Judgment— Tenant. June of 2009."

"Damn!" Morris rides, "You ain't paid no rent since then? You must be sitting on some serious paper."

"Ben," beams The Sergeant "Hold onto your seat. Here's an email sent 12/1/11—that's yesterday, at 1:06 pm; from S.A. Meyer, Attorney at Law to C. Scaringella. Dear Carmine, As I have stated, it's in your best financial interest to have this matter resolved by the end of the year, so I will

approach your tenant first thing next week and offer to settle for $75,000, with an agreement he vacate by the end of
next month. Sincerely—Hah! How much more awesome
could it get?"

Morris taunts, "Show me the Money! Hah! You rich
now, so find an apartment."

"Give him time to get used to the idea," asserts The
Sergeant, and keeps typing.

I hesitate. I vacillate, "I'm not sure what I'll do."

"Why not . . . move in with the girl?" prompts The
Sergeant.

I slight, "We only met last week."

Their eyes look up and glower. The perp will always lie.

"OK," I confess. "We had a thing a few years back.
And as much as I'd like us to pick right up again, she has
some issues with her ex. Not to mention a six-month-old
daughter."

The Sergeant scans the screen, "The ex won't be a problem. He's doing time in Canada for smuggling marijuana.
And word is he still owes the guys he got it from money."

"Look," I explain. "Doesn't matter how it seems. Love's
like a taxi with the light off. But you can't afford forever."

"Dude's a poet," chuckles Morris.

The Sergeant reads more from the screen. "Here's a
message she sent to her sister on Facebook: You remember
the man in my old building that I thought I was in love
with a few years ago? Well—now I know I was, so wish me
luck. I'm in love with Ben again."

Morris quips, "You in like Flynn!"

I ask, "So am I free to go?" Their eyes meet up and grin.
I stand.

The Sergeant says, "Ben. We're only one of seven exper-
imental subway crime prevention programs.

"What do the other six do?" I ask.

The elevator door shakes open behind me. I look down and see the bag. Morris says, "It's a knockoff."

The Sergeant waves, "Come back and see us."

Just like life, it was over much too soon. And just like life, there weren't any answers. But like that one-in-an-eight-million great New York moment, I didn't need one.

I couldn't wait to tell Lateef that there were angels on the bottom. And there, rising to the skin from the bowels of the city, I never had so much direction in my life.

ABOUT THE AUTHORS

CLAUS ANKERSEN is an intergalactic traveller working with multiple artistic expressions, amongst these live-literature and performance poetry. He has performed his literature and poetry in 14 countries around the world. His work is translated to Swedish, English, Polish and Malayalam, with Hindi and Ukrainian translations pending. Besides three collections of poetry and a poetry CD, Ankersen has contributed to numerous anthologies in Denmark as well as internationally.

RONALD H. BASS is the author of *The Velveeta Underground*, a collection of short stories and one-act plays published in 2006 as part of the EAA Signature Series. His story "Marcel Duchamp Inaugurates the Arts and Crap Movement" appeared in the Spring 2011 issue of the *Columbia Review*.

LAWRENCE BLOCK has been publishing award-winning crime fiction for over half a century. Most of his work is set in New York, and most of his own years have been spent within the five boroughs. His recent books include *A Drop of the Hard Stuff*, featuring Matthew Scudder, and *Getting Off*, featuring a very naughty young lady.

ADAM R. BURNETT is writer and theatre artist living in Crown Heights, Brooklyn. He is the co-founder and Artistic Director of Buran Theatre Company, who he has directed, performed, written and produced with since 2007. His performance works have been produced internationally and his literary writings have been published both in print and online.

DARLENE CAH was born and raised in Brooklyn, NY. She now lives in a place where there are more cows than cars. Her flash stories have appeared in *Staccato Fiction*, *Smokelong Quarterly* and *Mindprints*, among other journals. She has an MFA in Creative Writing from Queens University of Charlotte.

KEVIN DUPZYK is a neo-Luddite from Northern California. He was educated in Berkeley, CA, where he spent time as a Staff Reader with the *Berkeley Fiction Review*. He works in short fiction and the essay and recently returned home after three years in Boston, MA.

LISA FERBER is a prolific New York City writer and artist. She creates witty, warm and elegant pieces, influenced by her fascination with humanity. Her works exhibit an appreciation of the beauty and quirks of human behavior, as well as a compassion for its foibles. She invites her audience to come and play in her world.

KOFI FOSU FORSON was born in Accra, Ghana, migrated to New York with family in 1978. He has written and directed plays for the Riant Theater. His play *Alligator Pass* was nominated for the Arnold Weissberg Award. At The Eickholt Gallery he served as Press Coordinator, exhibited paintings and drawings of his "Muse" series. He currently writes for *Whitehot Magazine*.

JANET HAMILL is a the author of five books of poetry and short fiction, the most recent being *Body of Water* (Bowery Books, 2008). She is has read widely in the US and Europe and regularly performs with the band Lost Ceilings. Janet lives in the Hudson Valley, where she is and instructor at the North East Poetry Center's College of Poetry.

DAVID R. LINCOLN is the author of a novel, *Mobility Lounge* (Spuyten Duyvil, 2005), and the recipient of a Christopher Isherwood Fellowship. He lives in Brooklyn with his wife and son, and is at work on a new novel.

PETER MARRA is from Williamsburg, Brooklyn. Born in Brooklyn, he lived in the East Village, New York from 1979-1993 at the height of the punk/no wave movement. A surrealist and Dadaist, he was first published in *Maintenant 4* and has had approximately 50 poems published in the past year, including an interview in *Yes, Poetry*. Among his influences are Tristan Tzara, Paul Eluard, Edgar Allan Poe, Russ Meyer, and Roger Corman.

JANE ORMEROD is the author of the full-length poetry collection, *Recreational Vehicles on Fire* (Three Rooms Press, 2009), the chapbook *11 Films* (Modern Metrics/EXOT Books, 2008), and the spoken word CD *Nashville Invades Manhattan*. A new collection is due from Three Rooms Press in 2012. Born on the south coast of England, Jane now lives in New York City. She was a founding editor at Uphook Press, and is currently founding editor at Great Weather For Media.

PUMA PERL is a poet, writer and performance artist who has been widely published in journals and anthologies. She is the author of the award-winning chapbook, *Belinda and Her Friends*, and the full-length collection, *knuckle tattoos*; a second chapbook is due for publication in 2012. She is the co-creator of DDAY Productions and produces and curates shows in several venues in lower Manhattan and Brooklyn.

PEDRO PONCE is the author of *Homeland: A Panorama in 50 States*, published by Seven Kitchens Press. His short fiction has appeared previously in *Ploughshares*, *PANK*, *Arroyo Literary Review*, and the anthology *Sudden Fiction Latino*. He lives in Canton, NY, where he teaches writing and literary theory at St. Lawrence University.

LARISSA SHMAILO's poetry has appeared in the 10th anniversary issue of *Barrow Street*, the 10th anniversary issue of *Drunken Boat*, *Fulcrum*, *Gargoyle*, *The Unbearables Big Book of Sex*, and the Penguin anthology *Words for the Wedding*. Her books of poetry are *In Paran*, *A Cure for Suicide*, and *Fib Sequence*; her poetry CDs are *The No-Net World* and *Exorcism*, for which she won the 2009 New Century Music award for spoken word. Larissa first translated the Russian zaum opera *Victory Over the Sun*, debuted at the Brooklyn Academy of Music and archived at MOMA, and recently received honorable mention in the 2011 international Russian literary translators competition for the Compass Award.

EDITORS

PETER CARLAFTES is an NYC playwright, poet, and performer. He is the author of 12 plays, including a noir treatment of Knut Hamsun's *Hunger*, and his own celebrity rehab center spoof, *Spin-Dry*. Carlaftes has recently published three books: *A Year on Facebook* (humor), *Drunkyard Dog* (poetry) and *Triumph for Rent* (3 plays). He is co-founder and editor of Three Rooms Press.

KAT GEORGES is an NYC poet, playwright, performer and designer. Her full-length poetry collection, *Our Lady of the Hunger* will be released soon on Three Rooms Press. In New York since 2003, she has directed numerous Off-Broadway plays, curated poetry readings, and performed widely. She is co-founder and editor of Three Rooms Press.

books on
three rooms press

POETRY

by Peter Carlaftes
DrunkYard Dog
I Fold with the Hand I Was Dealt

by Ryan Buynak
Yo Quiero Mas Sangre

by Joie Cook
When Night Salutes the Dawn

by Thomas Fucaloro
Inheriting Craziness is
   Like a Soft Halo of Light

by Kat Georges
Our Lady of the Hunger
Punk Rock Journal

by Karen Hildebrand
One Foot Out the Door
Take a Shot at Love

by Matthew Hupert
Ism is a Retrovirus

by Dominique Lowell
Sit Yr Ass Down or You Ain't gettin
no Burger King

by B.R. Lyon
You Are White Inside

by Jane Ormerod
Recreational Vehicles on Fire

by Susan Scutti
We Are Related

by Jackie Sheeler
to[o] long

by The Bass Player from Hand Job
Splitting Hairs

by Angelo Verga
Praise for What Remains

by George Wallace
Poppin' Johnny

PLAYS

**by Madeline Artenberg &
Karen Hildebrand**
The Old In-and-Out

by Peter Carlaftes
Triumph For Rent (3 Plays)
Teatrophy (3 More Plays)

by Larry Myers
Mary Anderson's Encore
Twitter Theater

ANTHOLOGIES

Have a NYC
New York Short Stories

**Maintenant: A Journal of
Contemporary Dada Literature &
Art** *(annually since 2003)*

PHOTOGRAPHY-MEMOIR

by Mike Watt
mike watt: on and off bass

FICTION

by Ronnie Norpel
Baseball Karma & The Constitution
Blues

by Michael T. Fournier
Hidden Wheel

HUMOR

by Peter Carlaftes
A Year on Facebook

for complete current catalog, please email info@threeroomspress.com
three rooms press I new york, ny I www.threeroomspress.com

9 780983 581338